Jessie Knows
A Claire Burke Mystery
(Book 4)

by
Emma Pivato

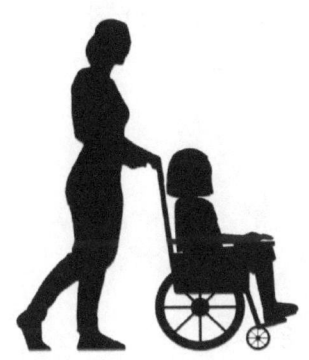

For information, email **Cozy Cat Press**, cozycatpress@gmail.com or visit our website at: www.cozycatpress.com

COZY CAT
PRESS

ISBN: 978-1-939816-76-4
Printed in the United States of America

10 9 8 7 6 5 4 3 2 1

This book is dedicated to my dear friend, Debbie Appleby. Debbie and I met when her son, Kent was two and our daughter, Alexis was three. Throughout their childhood years, we grieved, fumed, laughed and schemed together as we worked compulsively to make the world a better and more welcoming place for Kent, Alexis and other children dealing with profound, life altering disabilities. I know at a very deep level what it is like to have a blood sister.

Love you, Debbie

Prologue

Claire pushed Jessie's chair up the rear wheelchair ramp as fast as she could, and opened the school's back door to an unwelcome silence—meaning classes had already begun. Late again! The third time this year, and it was only the 16th of October. But this time there was a good reason. They'd been to the neurologist that morning for Jessie's six-month review and he'd been over an hour late in seeing them. Jessie had a severe seizure disorder along with all her other disabilities.

Alana Proux, Jessie's teacher, had made it abundantly clear that she did not like Jessie coming in late and disrupting the class for any reason. *Maybe I just should have taken her home for the rest of the day,* Claire thought. And, later, she very much wished that she had.

The school was a beautiful old building with a huge front atrium you could look out on from the second floor landing. That was where all the senior high and upper-level junior high classrooms were located. But the two grade seven rooms were by themselves on the main floor, down a long narrow hall that extended beyond the atrium and led to the back door—the only wheelchair accessible entrance. This greatly limited Jessie's opportunities to mingle with the majority of the students in the school and that upset Claire.

Jessie's sprawling, one-level elementary school had been so different—very warm and friendly with many opportunities for casual interactions with the other students. She'd been well accepted and even valued there. But Jessie was thirteen now and too old to remain in an elementary school—and this was where the school district had placed her.

The school was bad enough, but Jessie now shared her assistant, Pamela Burton, with an 11-year-old boy, and this assistant seemed to be primarily focused on keeping the boy, Nico, entertained so that he would not run away or have one of his frequent meltdowns. Therefore, Pamela had little time or energy left over for meeting Jessie's needs.

Claire had seen this pattern occurring every time she visited. But she'd have known anyway because of Jessie's mood when she came home in the afternoon. She was listless and restless and dull and, also, she was not sleeping well at night. That was exactly how Jessie responded when she had a nothing day and was largely ignored. This happened occasionally at home, as well, when there was a staffing breakdown and other family business took priority.

There were also Nico's frequent aggressive acts to worry about. Claire lived in fear of the day that he would lash out at Jessie as he'd already done with several other students in his class. *He'd be better off in a special class, for his sake and the sake of everybody else,* Claire thought. *Something terrible is going to happen one of these days.*

A wave of guilt washed over her. *If I hadn't been so preoccupied with the threat to Roscoe and the running of the home for him and Mavis and Bill this past year, I would have been more focused on Jessie's situation and I would have pushed harder for an individual assistant for her.* But when Claire recalled the long hard path they'd travelled to make that community living home a reality, and the many little successes they'd had along the way leading up to that moment, she felt a thrill of satisfaction.

First, there'd been the discovery that Jimmy, now the husband of her best friend, Tia, had a sister with severe disabilities in a Calgary institution. They'd finally convinced him to bring Mavis to Edmonton, and initially Jimmy had managed with her in his home, receiving some limited funding assistance for caretaking help.

Next, Marion McKay, whose autistic nephew, Bill, was in the same institution as Mavis, had decided to move to Edmonton to live with her only daughter, Hilda, because of Marion's deteriorating heart condition. And she brought Bill with her so he could be close by, since she was his legal guardian. That had created a whole additional pile of problems that were now resolved, thanks to a lot of hard work and risk on the part of Claire and Tia—especially Tia.

Then one day, when Claire had been discussing with Jimmy possible future living arrangements for Mavis and Bill, he'd told her that another young man from the Calgary institution would be moving to Edmonton with his parents. That was when Claire had had her brainwave about buying the house right across the street from Jimmy and Tia as a home for the three of them. Jimmy had called Roscoe's father and the rest—as they say—is history.

But Claire's moment of self-satisfaction passed and now her anger returned. Angela Arietti, Nico's mother, who'd seemed so helpful and generous at first, had turned out to be anything but. *She* was apparently the one driving the assistant Pamela Burton to focus primarily on Nico at Jessie's expense. All her fine talk when Claire had first met her about making sure that both Nico and Jessie got what they needed had been just that—a smokescreen to keep Claire from getting involved in the situation until it was too late.

"Spla-a-a-t!" Suddenly there was a very loud, wet sound. Claire and Jessie were just outside the classroom door at this point, but Claire kept moving towards the front lobby to see what had happened. When they reached it, she heard agitated voices above her and saw that people were leaning over the railing on the second-floor landing. Her gaze transferred down to the floor below it, and what she saw there made the hairs on the back of her neck stand up.

It was a body—a female body, lying face down, her long blond hair surrounded by a corona of blood and her neck at an impossible angle. A metallic smell filled the air around her and Jessie began to cry in a strange, keening way that Claire had heard only once before. She stood there numbly until Jessie's cries turned to screams. Then Claire whipped the wheelchair around and quickly headed back out the same door she'd just entered such a short time before. Jessie's assistant Pamela Burton was dead—and Claire did not think it had been an accident.

Chapter 1: Four Months Earlier

Claire was exhausted, but it was seven in the morning and, as was her habit, she'd snapped awake, waiting for Jessie to call out. Maybe she should check on her.

"Where are you going?" Dan asked, rolling over and pinning her down to the bed with his arms so she couldn't move.

"I can't sleep anymore. I might as well get up. Anyway, I thought I heard Jessie."

"It's Saturday; Jessie's still sleeping and Lydia will be here soon to look after her, so just lie there and rest awhile. You have to be worn out from all you've been through recently."

"I am, and I'm so glad things worked out the way they did—but I feel like there's still unfinished business."

Dan rolled his eyes. "Please tell me you're going to leave this *unfinished* business alone. Haven't we had enough drama in this house for awhile?"

"There's no more danger," Claire said defensively. "They're all in jail. But I still don't know the *reason* Sam was killed in the first place."

"Does it really matter at this point?" Dan asked.

"It matters to me," Claire muttered. "Sam was Roscoe's friend, and Roscoe has a good sense of people. He wouldn't have liked a really bad person."

During the past year, Claire had shut down her private practice as an interior decorator in order to take on a full-time position coordinating a home for three young adults with varying levels and types of disabilities.

One of the two men, Roscoe, had Down's syndrome but, like many people with this diagnosis, he actually understood a lot and was capable of employment with the right level of support. Claire had arranged a work placement for him in a restaurant and one day, on his way home from there, he'd witnessed a murder and had thus, become a target for the killer.

Claire and her best friend Tia, along with Tia's neighbor, Amanda Roche, and Claire's Aunt Gus, had then worked together to find the killer before he succeeded in his efforts to eliminate Roscoe.

That was the third such adventure the little group had been involved in and Claire was still nursing a stiff knee and a wrenched shoulder from a desperate effort to save Tia, who'd been caught by the killer while snooping. Dan and Tia's husband, Jimmy, had both been deeply frightened by the close calls both women had experienced and were very resistant to them having any further involvement in hunting for murderers.

Because of Claire's and Tia's actions, the murderer had been apprehended and was now safely in jail along with the murderer's associates. And there had been another positive outcome. As compensation for the suffering he'd experienced, Roscoe had been given the restaurant where he'd worked, plus an additional $30,000.00.

However, there were still some loose ends and Claire never liked loose ends. And today was the first day she'd have time to take care of these. "What are your plans for today?" she asked her husband innocently.

"I have to go into the office. Sorry. This new client I've been telling you about decided he wants a full-sized private bathroom built right into his office so he doesn't need to rely on the public ones in the hall. His whole project is a really big contract for us and I'm afraid I need to cater to his timeline and his demands. I'll probably have to be there most of the day."

"Oh, that's too bad," Claire said. "Well, business comes first, I guess."

Dan looked at her apologetically, but Claire was secretly happy about this turn of events, as it would give her the opportunity to do the follow-up work she was planning without any interference from Dan.

"Sounds to me like that client is creating a little love nest for himself, a home away from home, as it were," she added.

"That may be," Dan said brusquely, never one to gossip. "But if so, it's his business and not mine. I just need to redraw those specifications in order to give him what he wants."

Chapter 2: Claire Tidies Up

After Dan left for his office, Claire checked on Jessie who was doing range of motion exercises with her caretaker, Lydia, and then she made a phone call. She arranged to visit Iris, the mother of the dead boy Sam, and Sarah, Sam's 16-year-old sister. She took with her the former restaurant owner who'd told them about Sam refusing to sell drugs anymore at the school where a fifteen-year-old had died from an overdose. Sam had also threatened to go to the police if somebody else took his place and continued selling them. That apparently was the real reason he'd been killed. It was not because he'd stolen some of the drugs he was supposed to be selling, as they'd been led to believe.

After Claire told this story to Sam's relatives, she could see the looks of relief and pride on the faces of Sarah and Iris. Glancing around the barren, drafty room where they lived, she could also see their poverty. Claire realized that Sam's work selling drugs must have gone a long way towards supporting them when he was alive. She returned home feeling that it had been a good day's work. But she also felt sad for the financial state Sam's mother and sister were in.

Monday evening, while Claire was relaxing after dinner and mulling over ideas for decorating Roscoe's new restaurant, she received a phone call from a very excited Iris. According to Sam's mother, their doorbell had rung earlier that evening and when they'd answered the door, there was nobody there. However, they'd found a taped up shoebox addressed to them. When they opened it, they discovered it was full of money and when they counted the money, they found it came to $20,000.00!

"Wow! That's great! That should make your life easier!" Claire replied. *More laundered money,* she thought with concern, but it was certainly in a good cause.

Chapter 3: Renovating on a Shoe String

Claire's next big project was to help Roscoe and his family deal with the restaurant he'd inherited, formerly known as The Piccadilly Fish and Chips Shoppe. A building inspection had revealed no major structural problems, but some electrical upgrading was required and the kitchen fan needed to be replaced.

This left them with less than $15,000.00 to do the cosmetic upgrading and to purchase the materials necessary to turn the establishment into a Japanese-American fusion restaurant, as Roscoe wanted. His parents, Fuji and Yuna, and his sister-in-law, Hura, made out a list of necessities and, with help and suggestions from friends in the Japanese community, set about acquiring them.

Various Japanese tea sets and dishes that had been moldering for years in basements or in rarely frequented buffet units were offered up freely or for small sums of money. The owners' satisfaction came from seeing them pressed into proper use for once and in relishing the prospect of a new place to meet with friends and experience at least a small sample of the food and the atmosphere of the homeland they'd left behind.

Through these connections, Roscoe's uncle, Daisuke, the designated restaurant chef, was put in touch with a retired Japanese chef named Satou Botan who'd managed to bring his entire set of culinary knives with him when he left Osaka to come to Canada. Botan was unwilling to part with them because they represented his last link to his former life. However, when Daisuke invited him to give some suggestions about the layout of the kitchen and to take a part-time position as chef and perhaps share some of his recipes with him, Botan jumped at the offer and was quite happy to leave his knives in the kitchen for their joint use.

Then it was Claire's husband's turn to get involved. The building, itself, was square and unimaginative, and Dan struggled with developing a design that could give the space some grace and dignity and the Japanese ambience that was desired while still working within a very limited budget. He finally came up with a plan of half-walls that divided the space into four areas with two or three tables in each. As a concession to Westerners and those with disabilities, the tables would be at a regular height, but their graceful oval shapes, the simple chairs with their rounded backs and the delicate lamps hanging overhead would provide a gracious atmosphere in harmony with Japanese tastes. A tall, elegant, Tansu step-chest had been donated by an elderly Japanese lady going into an assisted living arrangement. Its placement just inside the front door blocked immediate visual access to the diners and set the tone for the restaurant.

Once Fuji and Daisuke had completed the necessary renovations, it was Claire's turn to work with Yuna and Hura in determining the color scheme and the appropriate table and window coverings. Claire purchased the necessary materials from various factory outlets and Tia and her mother then fashioned the tablecloths of crisp white polyester/cotton that required no ironing, and red polyester covers that did not stain and could be easily switched between settings as needed. The windows were adorned with semi-transparent sheers and deep, red side curtains of heavy velvet that hung well. Marisa worked many nights fashioning the sheers and drapes to their satisfaction, and Jimmy hunted down the appropriate rods for hanging them. The rods had elegant black knobs in the shape of curlicues on their ends that fit in with the overall décor.

The former owner had left the restaurant intact with its dishes, cutlery, glasses and kitchenware, but the heavy, cafeteria-style dishes did not suit the new character of the restaurant. Claire found an abundant supply of squared white Corelle dinnerware at a factory outlet, as well as a huge stack of durable but slender glasses deeply discounted because the line was being discontinued. Most Western restaurants were now favoring larger glasses, but these smaller, more delicate ones were exactly what this Japanese-themed restaurant required.

Yuna discovered a quantity of beautiful, white-lacquered chopsticks at a Japanese import store for a reasonable price and this left enough money in the budget for Claire to purchase good quality stainless steel flatware to accommodate Western diners.

Chapter 4: An Invitation and a Surprising Response

Finally, the restaurant was ready for a trial run and Roscoe, Daisuke, Yuna and Fuji invited the whole group for a complimentary meal and naming session as a thank you for all their assistance.

"Humph!" Tia said sourly to Claire. "It's little enough after all we've done to support Roscoe. Rightfully speaking, I think that restaurant should belong to all three of our people—not just Roscoe. And I'm not even sure how much Roscoe is going to benefit. Looks to me like Daisuke and Fuji and Yuna have just taken over. And Yuna is even talking about her grandsons getting jobs as servers there. It seems like they're all taking advantage of Roscoe's good fortune, but they're sure not sharing it around!"

Claire just looked at Tia thoughtfully for a minute before speaking. "I guess you've forgotten what it's like to be an immigrant, Tia—to come here and have nothing and to be treated like nothing. And then, if you were Japanese during World War II, to have whatever you did manage to acquire through hard labor be taken away from you and to be uprooted and placed in a makeshift camp far from the new home you'd established. It doesn't leave you feeling very charitable, I should imagine."

"But *they* weren't in any camps! They came here long *after* the war!"

"No, but there are older people in their community who were—and it becomes part of the cultural baggage that the whole group carries."

"I guess you might be right—but I still feel it would have been nice if they'd included the rest of us in their good fortune."

"What? So we could run some sort of little commune? This is the land of private enterprise. Remember?"

"Yes, but…"

"People give when they are given to, when they feel valued and like they belong. Look what happened to Marion's daughter, Hilda! Remember? She didn't want anything to do with helping Bill, even though she's his cousin and her mother's his guardian! All she seemed to be concerned about was not losing out on any of her inheritance! But she seems quite different now than when we first met her…more helpful and like she even enjoys helping out at times. Let's see what happens down the road and, meanwhile, let's not judge."

"How did you get so noble, Claire?" Tia said flippantly, but with a note of respect in her voice.

"I'm *not* noble, but I have noticed a change in some of my attitudes through the years. I think it has to do with Jessie. You can't know and care for someone like her day after day without rethinking some of your basic assumptions about life."

Chapter 5: A Trial Run and a Celebration

Claire and Dan, along with Tia, Jimmy and Tia's son, Mario, were the first guests to arrive at the restaurant the night of the big pre-opening celebration. Claire had struggled hard with deciding whether or not to bring Jessie, but Jessie's limited tolerance for noise, her frequent seizures and her unpredictable and often very vocal spells of unhappiness decided Claire against bringing her daughter. This night was too important to Roscoe and his family and the rest of them who'd invested so much time and energy into the restaurant venture to risk a major disruption.

Roscoe and his parents were there to greet them at the door. Roscoe was dressed in the tuxedo he'd worn for Jimmy's and Tia's wedding that Tia had worked so hard to salvage—firstly, from blood stains and, secondly, from the cold water bath to which Claire had subjected it. She'd used a special enzyme formula, and now there was only the faintest pink blush on the jacket arm where the bullet had hit Roscoe. Tia's mother, Marisa, had mended the hole in the jacket so cleverly that you couldn't even tell that it had ever been there. Claire doubted that any contemporary seamstress would have had that kind of skill—a dying art.

But the most challenging part of the restoration for Tia had been to undo the damage from the water bath that had shrunk the fabric and changed its texture. Fortunately, the pants hem had been previously raised on the inside to accommodate Roscoe's short, stocky frame and was able to be lowered to the right length.

The jacket had always been too long for his torso and was now actually a better fit. But the major problem was the loss of body and of the satiny sheen of the fabric. However, by adding liquid laundry starch to a final rinse, air drying the suit and then pressing fabric softener sheets lightly into the fabric with an iron on low heat, Tia had finally managed to mitigate much of the damage and to create a smooth enough surface on the pants so they could take and hold a sharp crease.

Roscoe stood before them now as their *maître de*, proud, business-like and dignified. He showed them to their seats, a special table set aside in their honor— because, without their diligent work, he and his family knew that this day would not have happened.

Soon the others arrived, Hilda and Marion first, and then the assistants, Tom and Emily, with Roscoe's roommates, Mavis and Bill. Gus and Amanda were next and a few minutes later, Roscoe's brother, Randy, and his family dragged in. Randy was looking cross because his boys had not been ready when they were supposed to be.

Daisuke and Botan were both in the kitchen that night, nervously preparing the dishes for the meal, with fumbling help from some of the group home staff who were assisting as servers. Botan was something of a Sushi expert so the group was served a variety of delicious sushi followed by various beef, fish and vegetable dishes with rice. Desert was a choice of a simple fruit plate or the restaurant's signature coconut cream pie. The latter had been special-ordered from a near-by bakery and the servers had rather clumsily put together the fruit plates because the two chefs had had all they could do to manage the rest of the meal.

The meal was a wonderful success, and generous compliments and a variety of toasts followed it. Fuji then suggested that they begin work on the naming process. There was a strong group feeling about naming the restaurant after Roscoe and various suggestions were offered up such as *Roscoe's Retreat* and *Roscoe's Restaurant*. But Claire's all-time favorite in the absurdity category was the suggestion from Aunt Gus of *Roscoe's Roost*!

At that point, Roscoe himself interjected, reminding Claire once again of what a nice man he was. "Naw, ony Woscoe! Naw wight. Eviebody hep." Claire had noted on previous occasions that Roscoe's enunciation became even worse when he was excited or when he was trying to participate in a rapidly moving conversation.

"What name would you suggest then, Roscoe?"

"You call us *The Thwee Musketeehs*. We could call dis place dat!"

"Not very Japanese!" Daisuke had countered.

"We can say it in Japanese, too, Daisuke Ojo."

"Hmmm," Fuji murmured, and then he pulled out a piece of paper and began scribbling. A minute later, he showed his proposed sign to the group:

The Three Musketeers
三銃士

Everyone stopped talking at that point and simply stared at Fuji's drawing. Randy spoke for all of them then. "I think that's *it!*" he said. "That does it for *me!*" Everyone else agreed and it was done. They then drank a toast to *The Three Musketeers* restaurant.

Chapter 6: An Unwelcome Transfer

With all the excitement of getting the restaurant ready for operation and Claire's ongoing responsibility to ensure that Roscoe, Bill and Mavis had what they needed in terms of personal support and appropriate daytime activities, Claire had not had much time left-over to worry about Jessie. She was just grateful that Jessie had such a great school situation with the same caring and conscientious assistant for the past three years now, who understood her and made sure her needs were met. But recently, Jessie's assistant, Mary, had informed Claire that she and her husband were planning to move and that she would not be available to work with Jessie during the next school year.

Claire was worrying about this unfortunate turn of events and wondering when the school planned to advertise for a new assistant—and if she could be in on the hiring. However, the letter she found waiting for her one evening when she came home from work gave her a great deal more to worry about. It was from the school board informing Jessie's parents that because she was now thirteen, she needed to be placed in a more age-appropriate setting, and a junior/senior high school near her current school had been identified *as* that setting. Equally concerning was the school board's decision that Jessie could no longer be funded for an individual assistant, but would need to share one with an eleven-year-old boy who would be attending this new school in the coming year.

Claire and Dan spent a very anxious evening mulling the situation over. They looked up the new school, Newton Heights, on-line and discovered that it was a two-story building. Claire phoned the board office the next day and spoke to Ellen Watters, the consultant assigned to the transfer, about the accessibility issue.

"Don't worry about that," Ellen assured her. "There's a freight elevator that goes from the main floor to the basement where the student lunchroom is so Jessie will be able to use it if she has lunch with the other students—and both grade seven classrooms are on the main floor so there's no access problem there. The school is installing a ramp this summer at the back entrance to make it wheelchair accessible. There are only two steps there so it should be quite easy to push Jessie's chair up and down the ramp."

"But what about next year when she's in grade eight?"

"They may extend the freight elevator to the second floor, but so far there's not enough money in the budget for that."

"Oh, and I suppose if they don't have the money then Jessie can just be moved to another school. It's not as if it matters, shuffling around people like her!" Claire said sarcastically.

"No," Ellen replied in measured tones, obviously used to dealing with irate parents. "There's always the possibility that she could remain in grade seven a second year and, by that time, for sure there will have been enough time and money to install the elevator."

Claire hung up the phone soon after, feeling angry and upset—and ultimately helpless. But the one good thing that had happened during the call was that Ellen had agreed to pass on Claire's phone number to the other parent, Nico's mother. And the young man's mother—Angela Arietti—phoned her the very next evening. They talked for about an hour, neither of them seeming able to get their words out fast enough, and it soon became evident that the two of them shared many of the same concerns.

"Don't worry about the elevator issue!" Angela said in conclusion. "I'm not letting this go. I don't give up and I generally get my way in the end. I will personally see to it that that's dealt with quickly. After all, it affects Nico, too! If Jessie is restricted to one floor, then so is he, since their assistant can't be in two places at once."

"What about the assistant?" interjected Claire. "Is she going to be able to cope with both of them?"

"Oh, yes, her name's Pamela Burton. I've met her and she seems pretty competent. And it's not like they are *both* in wheelchairs. Nico does not require any help with personal care, so that should make it easier."

When Claire asked what Nico was like, Angela replied, "He's a great kid! He just has a few learning problems and is a little on the rambunctious side."

Claire felt much better after this call and decided there was really not much more she could do about the situation anyway. She'd just have to wait and see how things worked out. She went back to dealing with all her other concerns and the summer passed swiftly.

Chapter 7: Murder Changes Everything

After Claire returned home with Jessie on the day of her assistant Pamela Burton's violent death, they both just sat in the kitchen for fifteen minutes or so, each trying to come to terms with what had happened in their own way. Finally, Claire realized that Jessie's head was drooping, so after attending to her bathroom needs, she put her down for a nap.

Claire was just sitting down with a cup of tea, to mull over the situation further when the doorbell rang.

"Inspector McCoy!" Claire exclaimed when she opened the door. "Come in!" Claire was shocked to see the detective, but not really that surprised if she actually asked herself. After all, a woman had just died under suspicious circumstances and he was probably investigating. Claire had been there at the time of the assistant's fall to her death, so McCoy was just probably coming over to get her perspective of the events. Claire knew from sad experience that her best tactic when dealing with this man was to be calm and welcoming.

Once the policeman was seated and Claire had offered him some tea and left-over coffee cake, McCoy began his questioning.

"Your daughter's assistant fell to her death this afternoon, Ms. Burke. You were in the school at the time, I understand, so you are either a witness *or* you were involved. And you left the scene afterwards, which you know you had no business doing!"

Claire had thought she and McCoy had built up some rapport during their last murder investigation together, but now it sounded like he was back to his old, crusty self. *I better be very careful what I say and how I say it,* she thought. "I'm sorry, Inspector, but Jessie was screaming at that point. You can ask the others who were there. I *had* to get her home." Claire marveled again at how often Jessie had provided a convenient excuse for her actions.

McCoy seemed to accept this response and went on with his interrogation. "Why were you just arriving at the school at that time of the day with Jessie?"

Claire explained about Jessie's neurology appointment, sure that he'd already been told about that by Jessie's teacher.

"Where exactly were you, Ms. Burke, when Ms. Burton fell?"

"Just outside Jessie's classroom, about to go in."

"Did anybody see you there?" he asked, looking ominous.

"No. Class had already started. Nobody was in the hallway. I hadn't opened the classroom door yet."

"Did *you* see or hear anything unusual at that time?"

"No—just the noise when the body hit the floor." Claire gulped and then added, "I didn't even hear a scream. When I heard the noise, I just headed towards the lobby to see what had happened."

"What about afterwards? Did you notice anything unusual when you reached the lobby? Was anybody acting oddly, for instance?"

"No, nothing," Claire replied firmly.

"You must have seen something," McCoy insisted.

Claire just shook her head. She suddenly felt very weary. "I was way down the hallway, Inspector, as I told you, outside the door to Jessie's classroom when it happened. All I heard was this horrible *spl-a-at* sound and, by the time I reached the lobby, there was a bunch of people hanging over the railing, looking down. I couldn't even tell who all was there."

"Where was Ms. Burton's other student at the time? This. . .uh. . .Nico?" he asked.

"I understand that he was at home today—reportedly with a bad cold—and, I assume, his mother, Mrs. Arietti, was at home with him. He could hardly be left alone. I don't understand, Inspector. Why are you questioning me about this? Wasn't it an accident?"

"No, Ms. Burke, we don't believe it was. We have every reason to believe that Ms. Burton was pushed— that she was murdered."

Claire's heart flipped and no words would escape her mouth.

Just then, Jessie called out, giving signs of waking up, and McCoy took his leave.

Surely, not again! Not another murder! thought Claire.

Claire gave Jessie her afternoon medication, placed her daughter in her reclining chair with her vibrating cushion and sat down to enjoy a cup of tea and to consider the situation. Sad and upsetting as it was that this murder had happened, Claire knew that her primary focus right now had to be on finding a substitute assistant for Jessie and Nico. *What to do?*

Claire allowed her mind to wander, considering all possibilities. She was still mulling it all over when Jessie's home assistant arrived at 3:30 to do the evening work with her until 8:00. And then it came to her!

"Lydia, I have something to tell you," Claire said, and explained what had happened. Lydia was predictably very shocked. She'd worked with Pamela Burton at the beginning of the school year to orient her to Jessie's needs, routine and signals, so she knew her.

"Would you consider going into the school and covering Pamela's position until they can get somebody else?" Claire asked.

After thinking it over for several minutes, Lydia agreed. "It would be a good experience to work in a school for awhile, and I'm pretty sure I could handle Nico." Claire had used Lydia as a sounding board on many school days when she'd visited there and had been frustrated by what was happening. And Lydia had met Nico at the beginning of September when she'd spent two days at the school orienting Pamela on how to care for Jessie and read her nonverbal signals.

"My mother never tolerated any nonsense from my little brother who was a bit like Nico, so I know what I have to do to keep him in line," Lydia added.

One problem solved. Now for the next one, Claire thought. She called the school and spoke to Jessie's teacher, Alana Proux. As she suspected, both the teacher and the principal, Gustaf Lennon, had also been feeling rather desperate about the situation and they were open to listening to Claire's idea for a temporary solution. And they also recognized that the bigger challenge they faced was to provide support for Jessie because of her high level of dependency and lack of a formal communication system. A totally new assistant could come in and work with Nico under the teacher's guidance without too much problem, but not with Jessie.

"Have Lydia come in in the morning with Jessie, Claire," Alana said. "I'll call Angela and ask her to keep Nico home tomorrow one more day to give Lydia a chance to adjust to the school situation. He may still be sick anyway. Please send in copies of Lydia's references, criminal record check and CPR training certificate in a sealed envelope with her so we have them on file. I'll clear it from here with Mr. Lennon and he can deal with the school board. I'm sure they'll go along with it if Lydia is all that you say she is."

Claire agreed, hung up the phone gleefully and told Lydia. "I will still stay until eight tonight," Lydia said, "and I can probably do tomorrow evening, but after that you'll be on your own. How are you going to manage?"

"Lydia, we'll manage. You have *no* idea what a relief it will be to me to have somebody in the school who actually cares about Jessie and who'll do the job properly. This fall has been hell!"

"I know," Lydia said soberly. "I'm sorry."

Claire jumped on the note of sympathy she heard in Lydia's voice. "If I can get somebody to take your place here and you find you can manage the situation with Nico at school, would you consider taking on the job permanently if the school agrees?"

"Possibly," Lydia said thoughtfully. I'm just finishing off the last course in nursing that I can do online, and I plan to register at Grant MacEwan University next fall to complete my degree. In the mean time, I need to earn enough money to pay my tuition, so full time work would be great! But I'll have to see how it goes there."

"Of course," Claire said absently, already moving on in her mind to the next step.

Chapter 8: Calling in the Troops

The next morning, Claire was able to leave for Roscoe's home as usual. She called it Roscoe's home because, in her mind, he was the one she worked with all day while the other two residents—Mavis and Bill— were off at their day programs.

Once Bill and Mavis had gone off on their special DATS buses to their day programs, Claire settled Roscoe in front of the computer purchased for his home program to work with him on some exercises. Roscoe had demonstrated some interest and facility with numeration, and she was hoping to develop his skills to the point where he could do some simple cashiering at his restaurant.

Once Roscoe was working away, Claire sat down with a cup of coffee and considered an idea that she'd been mulling over. But Claire never liked to think too much. She liked to act!

Picking up the phone, she invited Aunt Gus and Amanda over for coffee and a visit. The two older ladies lived together across the street from the group home and next door to Tia and Jimmy. Aunt Gus had moved to Edmonton from Calgary shortly after her best friend, Marion MacKay had left. Marion had a heart condition but she was legally responsible for her nephew, Bill, who was autistic and had lived in an institution. Marion wanted to be close to her daughter, Hilda, and had moved to Edmonton quite suddenly when an opening came up for Bill in an institutional setting there, although in the end, that had not worked out very well.

Always fiercely independent and declaring that she needed nothing from anybody, Gus had suddenly realized then that she was alone in Calgary. She had decided to move, and called Amanda in Edmonton. They had formed a close relationship two years earlier while they had been working together to identify a possible murderer when Gus had been visiting Claire.

Amanda invited Gus to share her home and, much to Claire's surprise, given Gus's rather self-centered nature, Gus agreed and now she and Amanda and their respective cats seemed to be getting along quite well. Both Claire and Tia had been amused to see how Amanda had kept Gus and her cats in line, setting certain limits in place—and how in some areas, she had meekly acceded to them.

By the time Gus and Amanda arrived at the house, Claire had coffee and plum cake on the table. Nettie, the new night assistant for Jessie, had made the cake, following a recipe taken from Jean Parés *Company's Coming* cookbook *Cakes*, a housewarming present from Tia.

Claire told the two elderly ladies what had happened at Jessie's school the day before, and Gus and Amanda were both shocked and worried for Jessie. Claire explained the arrangement she'd made for Lydia to go in to Jessie's school and replace the dead assistant, and they looked appropriately relieved. Then Claire broached her idea.

"I really can't manage at home without evening support and Lydia can't do both. I have to find somebody else and you know how hard *that* is." Gus and Amanda both nodded their heads in agreement.

"Do you have anybody in mind?" Amanda asked.

"There is one person," Claire said thoughtfully. "Karen Day, the lunch person at the school—but I can't really ask her to leave there and take care of Jessie unless I find a replacement for her. It would totally wreck my relationship with the school and it would be very unethical on my part."

"I see," Amanda said.

"I *see,*" Aunt Gus said.

"What are you thinking, Aunt Gus?" Claire asked innocently.

Aunt Gus cleared her throat and looked sideways at Amanda. "I was thinking that maybe if Karen is willing to take the evening job with Jessie, Amanda and I could help you out with the lunch thing. We could take the job on jointly and then at least one of us should be able to go every school day."

"Wow! I never thought of that!" Claire exclaimed. "Would you *really* consider it? It wouldn't be too *much* for you?"

Aunt Gus harrumphed. "We are not at death's door *yet*!"

"What do *you* have to say, Amanda?" Claire asked.

"It could work," she replied laconically. "But you shouldn't feel so guilty about asking Karen to help out with Jessie. Finding the school replacement for Jessie and Nico on such short notice was a really big thing! If push comes to shove, the teachers could handle the lunchroom for a couple of weeks." After a pause, she added, "We could agree to take it on temporarily and still get the school to advertise the position. Then if they like us and we like the job, we could stay on, but if not, we could hang in until they found a good replacement. I'm willing to commit to that much."

"Well, I'm very grateful—but there's one thing that worries me. A murderer is loose in that school."

"And that's *just* why we need to be there!" Gus crowed. "We can snoop around, meet people, and ask questions."

"It *would* be really good to have inside contacts in the school so we could find out who's behind this murder," Claire said thoughtfully, "but there *is* danger, so you'd have to be very subtle in asking questions," Claire warned, looking pointedly at Gus.

"Oh, we'll be careful, won't we, Amanda?"

"*You* be careful, Gus! I'm *always* careful—and I'm not interested in having to rescue you again!" Amanda was alluding to an earlier adventure where she'd saved Gus from a knife-wielding drug dealer.

"I know," Gus said soberly. "And I remember what happened to Tia last time."

Roscoe interrupted at that moment because he'd completed his math exercises and he wanted to show Claire the score the computer had automatically provided.

Gus and Amanda went home and Claire carried on with her morning's work with Roscoe—but she didn't like loose ends. At 11:30, she informed Roscoe that they were going to eat their lunch at Jessie's school, something they sometimes did to keep Jessie company and to provide another social opportunity for Roscoe.

Chapter 9: More of Claire's Persuasive Tactics

Once Roscoe and Claire had settled in at the lunch table with Jessie and Lydia, Claire watched for an opportunity and when Karen, the lunch lady, was alone, she left Roscoe with Lydia and Jessie and went to talk to her.

"Hi, Karen. You heard what happened to Pamela? I guess it happened just after you left yesterday?"

"Yes," she replied soberly. "It's unbelievable. I don't really feel safe here anymore. I'm surprised you could convince Lydia to come work here."

"I'm very grateful that she agreed. I don't know what we would have done otherwise. Of course, now we have no help at home," Claire added.

"Well, it shouldn't be too hard to get somebody else. Jessie is a nice girl. It would be a pleasure to work with her."

"Actually, it's not as easy as you think. Not too many people are interested in working 4 to 8 weekdays and 8 to 4 on Saturdays."

"Well, those would be perfect hours for me. As you know, I have classes at Grant MacEwan downtown at 9 and 10 every day, and sometimes it's a real struggle to get here by 11:30, in time for the lunch hour. Besides, it would be nice some days to just stay there and use their library. Also I could sure use the extra hours. This job doesn't pay much."

"Well, I'd give you the job in a minute if you were interested. I think you'd be really good with Jessie!"

"I'd love to do it," Karen said, wistfully. "But I couldn't leave the school just like that—not after what just happened. It would be too disruptive for everybody."

"Well, I happen to know somebody—two people actually, older ladies looking for a job like this—and they live nearby. If the school checked them out and was okay with it, then would you do it? I did the school a big favor by giving up Lydia so she could work here. They *owe* me one!"

"Do you really think they'd see it that way?"

"Let me go talk to Mr. Lennon right now and I'll get right back to you. Don't *go* anywhere!"

"Okay," Karen said, looking kind of dazed at how fast events were moving. But then she really didn't know Claire very well.

After a quick word with Lydia to stay in the lunchroom with Roscoe and Jessie, Claire headed briskly to the principal's office and caught him just as he was about to leave for an appointment downtown. He grudgingly agreed to see Claire briefly, but indicated his time was very limited. She explained the situation to him, stressing her sacrifice and the excellence of the proposed applicants. He agreed to meet with them at three that afternoon when he was sure he'd be back in the office. Claire left, collected Roscoe and the two of them marched back to the group house triumphantly, stopping to see Gus and Amanda first to tell them the news.

"That only gives me an hour to get ready and I haven't done my hair today!" Gus complained. Maybe we should call and arrange the appointment for tomorrow."

"No!" Claire said, more harshly than she meant to. "Please, Aunt Gus. Just wear your wig. You look very nice with it. I really need to get this settled. Too much has happened." She sat down abruptly at the table and put her head in her hands—and this time she wasn't acting.

Roscoe nervously patted Claire on the shoulder and Amanda placed a glass of orange juice in front of her. "I bet you were so busy wheeling and dealing that you didn't get around to eating your lunch, right?"

Claire nodded numbly.

"*Fine!* I'll go get ready. Excuse me, if I don't hang around and visit," Gus said, and she left the room abruptly.

Claire and Roscoe went back to Roscoe's house shortly after, and Claire half-heartedly worked through some grammar questions with him while she waited for Gus and Amanda to phone about the results of the interview. The phone rang at five minutes to four.

"We got the job!" Gus crowed. "Amanda and I are going in tomorrow to work with Karen and then we start on our own on Monday. We'll go in together at first to support each other, and then we'll take turns or both go in when we feel like it. And if we're both there together and one of us wants a break, we're welcome to use the staff room and have free coffee and cookies. That will be a good opportunity to talk to other staff and pick up information."

"That's wonderful!" Claire exclaimed. "But just remember what I said about being careful."

By the time the phone call ended, Emily had arrived to meet the DATS bus, as Mavis would be home shortly. Tom arrived a couple of minutes later. He and Emily were both part-time students, able to cover the afternoon shifts during the week when Bill, who was autistic and able to speak only about 100 words, and Mavis, who was nonverbal and confined to a wheelchair, arrived back from their day programs.

Tom and Emily worked evenings 4 to 11, Mondays to Fridays at the home. Claire had been lucky to find them. Not many people were willing to take a shift like that where they didn't have a single weekday evening free. Since Claire had agreed to manage the home that she and Tia and their families had set up for Mavis, Bill and Roscoe a year ago, staffing it had been the major problem. But after some false starts, they'd found a few solid people they could count on.

Tom and Emily also monitored Roscoe who was higher functioning than his roommates, but still required some support. But, since the restaurant had opened, Roscoe was now picked up by DATS at 4:30 on Wednesday, Friday and Saturday afternoons and taken there. He served as *maître d,*' cheerfully greeting friends, family and strangers alike.

Claire usually stayed until five at the home to finish up paperwork, but now she felt quite exhausted and decided to leave early that day. Even by her standards, the wheeling and dealing she'd done in the past 24 hours had been a bit over the top. She went across the street to Tia's home to tell her about all the new arrangements and perhaps to revel a bit in Tia's admiration for her ingenuity.

Tia was simultaneously impressed and repelled by all of Claire's reported machinations. "Sometimes I don't know what to make of you, Claire," she said. It's a good thing you don't have anti-social tendencies because you definitely have a conniving mentality!" But to soften her words, she added, "I'm really glad you were able to work things out for Jessie. I know how difficult that staffing situation has been at times. "But have you cleared all this with Nico's mother?"

"No," Claire groaned. "But surely she won't object. She must be able to see that it's in Nico's best interests as well."

However, as it turned out, that was not how Angela saw it at all.

Chapter 10: A Nasty Conversation

"Who gave *you* the authority to go ahead and arrange the school assistant for *my* child?" Angela Arietti shrilled over the phone early the next morning.

"And what about Jessie? *She's* the one who needs an assistant with specialized training, not Nico. Did you *really* want to have him home with you for the next two weeks—minimum—while they advertised, interviewed, checked references, hired and trained somebody?"

"Well, just don't think that because she worked with Jessie first that she can neglect Nico!" Angela snarled.

Claire thought this was rich coming from the woman who'd bullied poor Pamela Burton into spending the lion's share of her time and attention with Nico at Jessie's expense—but she said nothing.

"*I'll* talk to Lydia," Angela added. "Just because she knows how to look after Jessie doesn't mean she'll know anything about Nico's needs. I will make damn *sure* that she understands how to deal with him so that he doesn't get short-changed. Don't think you're going to pull the wool over *my* eyes!"

Claire, a master of clichés herself, was suddenly aware of how tired they could sound. But all she said was, "I'm sure Lydia will learn quickly what's best for Nico. She's a very sincere and intelligent person, and a hard worker. She's going into Nursing at Grant MacEwan next fall."

"That's just it!" Angela griped. "That's *not* the mentality Nico needs. He needs somebody playful and energetic—not a Florence Nightingale type!"

"Look, Angela. I'd love to keep discussing this with you, but I have to get to work now. Why don't you drop by the school today and see for yourself how Lydia is doing with Nico. Maybe it won't be as bad as you think."

Knowing Angela, she probably won't get there much before noon and Aunt Gus and Amanda will be spending the lunch hour observing Karen. Maybe they can listen in on what she says to Lydia, and then I'll be better prepared to counteract it, Claire thought.

That evening, Lydia came to work with Jessie at home for the last time. Claire had arranged for Karen to come as well so Lydia could train her. After a couple of hours, it was clear that Karen was catching on quickly. Jessie was now securely strapped into her wheeled standing-frame and Karen was running the massager up and down her back. Lydia was able to leave them alone so she and Claire could have a private talk.

Lydia assured Claire that Karen would be able to handle the essentials at the end of the evening and any fine tuning Claire could do. Claire thanked her and then asked, "How did things go today at school, Lydia? You were working with Nico for the first time and I heard that his mother came in?"

"Uh-huh," Lydia said. "What a piece of work!"

"Who? Nico or his mother?"

"Both, actually—but Nico I can handle. I'm not so sure about his mother."

"Why? What did she do?"

"It's more what she *didn't* and *doesn't* do. She has all these strategies she's devised for working around him and keeping him diverted and entertained and she expects me to use them. But she never wants to face the real issue."

"Which is?"

"That he's constantly bullying her—and, like all bullies, he's unhappy, and therefore never really satisfied no matter what she does. And she's too intimidated to deal with him directly so she vents her frustration by turning around and bullying others."

"Wow!" Claire said. "I sort of felt that but I couldn't put it in words like you've done. How are you going to handle the situation?"

"By developing a tight schedule and by collaborating closely with the teacher."

"I haven't found the teacher to be very cooperative––and she certainly hasn't taken much interest in Jessie."

"She's confused and over-whelmed by the situation––and Angela's gotten to her, too."

"What do you mean?"

"Nico likes to run away when you're not paying attention to him all the time. I think he knows that you'll have to drop everything and run after him then and he likes that. Angela told the teacher that if he ever got away and something happened to him, she'd sue the teacher and the assistant for negligence—and she mentioned that she had the legal connections to do it and make sure it sticks!"

"So what did the teacher—Alana—tell you to do?"

"She said I was never to let him out of my sight."

"What about attending to Jessie's needs?"

"Alana thinks you fuss too much over Jessie, that she's happy just sitting there, and that keeping her on a regular toileting schedule is absurd. I should just change her when I have to and at those times I'm to make sure that Nico is in class with her and that I come back with Jessie as quickly as I can."

"And Jessie's exercises?" Claire asked with deceptive mildness, making a heroic effort to keep her temper in check.

"Again, she thinks that it's kind of pointless and far too time-consuming. Also, she says that exercising Jessie does not qualify as education, and schools are educational institutions."

"I see," Claire said slowly—through gritted teeth. "And I suppose playing hide and seek all day with a spoilt brat *is* educational."

"Don't worry, Claire. I have a plan."

"What are you going to do?"

"I'm already doing it."

"What?"

"This afternoon, I contacted the Complex Needs Unit at the School Board Office downtown and informed myself of what services they could offer for somebody like Nico. Then I had a private word with Mr. Lennon."

"On your first day there—and without talking to the teacher first? She's the one who's supposed to be directing *you,* in case you don't know yet how the system works."

"When I mentioned the idea to Alana, she just shook her head. She said she had already suggested to Angela that they get the Complex Needs Unit involved but Angela had been dead set against it. Angela believes that Nico's negative behaviors have to do with his condition and can't be fixed. She feels we will only upset him and make him feel unloved and unwanted if we try."

"What did the principal say?"

Lydia turned to Claire triumphantly. "He said that he was completely fed up with Nico rampaging through the school and would do whatever it took as long as it was in his power to get him under control."

"He hasn't done much so far!" Claire retorted.

"Leave it to the Complex Behaviors Unit," Lydia said, smirking. "I know what they do there and they've brought worse kids than Nico into line."

"How do you know that?"

"My brother has told me some things about their strategies."

"I thought you said your brother *had* a behavior problem."

"Not my *younger* brother—my older one, Eric. He's a psychologist attached to that unit."

"You never said!"

"You never asked," Lydia said smugly.

Just then, they heard Jessie cry out that it was time for her to get out of the standing frame. Lydia went back to help Karen attend to her and go through the rest of the evening's routine. Claire read for a while and then went to bed. She was completely wrung out by all that had happened in the past two days. But she also felt happy and hopeful about Jessie's school situation for the first time that year.

Tomorrow, I can start focusing on the murderer, Claire said to herself just before she dozed off.

Chapter 11: Let the Games Begin

Monday morning Claire and Gus arrived at the school at 11:15 to get organized for taking up their new lunchroom supervision duties. The junior high students had lunch from 11:30 to 12:30 and the senior high students ate from 12:30 to 1:30. The lunchroom was in the basement, well-insulated from the classrooms, so the staggered lunch hours didn't cause a disturbance for the students not on break. There was a work elevator—the only elevator in the building—running from the main floor to the basement so that equipment and supplies could be transported downstairs. That was the elevator Jessie had to use to access the lunchroom and her teacher and assistant had the elevator code. Claire had also asked for and been given the code to pass onto Gus and Amanda so they didn't have to use the stairs. Gus's knees were not very good.

Principal Gustaf Lennon himself came into the lunchroom to introduce the students to Ms. Roche and Ms. Kalline (Gus and Amanda), and he followed that up with his usual request to be polite and respectful and to behave appropriately. The students soberly acceded to this request—until he left the room and enough time had passed for him to be no longer in hearing distance.

The first incident occurred when one large, bullish-looking junior high boy blew a big bubble with his gum that finally popped. His friends snickered and there was a general light titter throughout the room. Gus looked very uncomfortable, clearly not knowing what to do. But Amanda just said tersely, "Get rid of that."

"If you say so, ma'am," he replied with false deference—and he slowly and deliberately removed the gum from his mouth and stuck it under his seat.

"In the garbage," Amanda said, shaking the pail in his direction. He pretended not to hear her and there was more laughter.

Amanda got up slowly, hoisted the garbage pail and brought it over to him. "Now!" she said. Nothing happened. Amanda picked up the boy's lunch, still neatly packed in the bag from his table and returned with it and the pail to her table.

"Hey! You can't do that. It's mine. I'm going to tell the principal!"

"Go ahead!" Amanda said. "But you can have it back if you like. All you have to do is put your gum in the garbage first."

The boy fidgeted and sulked in his chair while those around him started eating their lunches. There was no laughing now and the peanut gallery appeared to be missing in action. Amanda ignored him and started talking to Gus who seemed to be transfixed by the whole situation. This, of course, did not fit with Amanda's strategy and in order to breathe life back into Gus, she began talking to her about her favorite subject—herself.

"I like that dress on you, Gus, and whatever you have under it *really* does it justice! It gives you the figure of a 20-year-old!" Slight exaggeration there, but Amanda decided it was necessary.

"Yes, I'm rather pleased with it, and my new *Spanx* corset is great—and comfortable, too! I hardly know I'm wearing it!"

Amanda rather doubted that, as she noticed Gus was only mincing away at her lunch. She searched frantically for something else to say that would keep Gus engaged once the soothing balm of her compliment had worn off, but she noted out of the corner of her eye that the *gum bully,* as she had taken to calling him privately, was approaching.

"We should discuss Saturday night," Amanda said, turning to Gus. Gus raised her eyebrows but the boy was now at their table. He held the gum in his hand and threw it in the garbage pail. Amanda picked up his lunch and held it out to him, but before giving it to him she asked mildly, "What's your name, son?"

"Why? Are you planning to report me?" he asked with some of his old pugnacity.

"No-o. Just curious, that's all."

"Ed." Amanda raised her eyebrows. "Ed Hale."

"Oh. What grade are you in, Ed?"

"Grade 9."

"You'll be in senior high next year. Have you figured out yet what you want to do when you graduate?"

"What do *you* care?"

"Just curious, like I said. You're certainly big and strong looking. I bet people think you're older than you are. Are you good at sports?"

"I like football some." Ed was twitching back and forth by this time and his cheeks were flushed red. He was obviously keenly aware that the rest of his group was taking it all in, his little chat with the *enemy*.

Amanda noted this. She was very observant. "Look at me, holding you up when you want to eat your lunch. I'm sorry. Here you are." she said and she handed Ed his lunch. "Nice chatting with you."

Ed muttered an almost inaudible *thanks* and returned quickly to his chair.

Gus turned to Amanda, goggle-eyed and opened her mouth to speak. But Amanda stepped firmly on her foot under the table and turned to face her with a warning scowl. Gus got the message and Amanda went back to reading her book.

The rest of the lunch hour and the senior lunch hour went quietly. The second group had obviously heard something from the first one, so after the principal came in and gave his little speech again, they ate their lunches and talked quietly with each other. If there was any horseplay it was very subdued and Amanda did not deign to notice.

When Gus and Amanda returned home from their lunchroom duties, they stopped in to see Claire and Roscoe at the group home. Gus regaled them with the story of how Amanda had squelched the troublemaker and Amanda could not keep a tiny smile off her face. She had to acknowledge to herself that it was nice to be the center of attention for once.

Chapter 12: Collecting Clues and Strategizing

Claire found the story very amusing and regarded Amanda with appreciation. But her mind was already bent on solving the murder. "Did you see anything or anyone suspicious there?" she asked.

"Well, I don't think the murderer is likely to be one of the students, and that's who we were stuck spending our time with," Gus replied.

"May I remind you that this was *your* idea, Gus!" Amanda responded caustically.

"I just think there's no point in both of us sitting there for two hours. One of us could be moving around and talking to the teachers and the janitor, for example. I wouldn't mind doing that since you seem to be so good at managing the kids."

"Uh-huh," was all Amanda replied—but Gus got the message.

"Fine! You do one hour and I'll do the other. Maybe I should take the older ones. They seem to respond to me better." Gus was referring to the one student who'd asked to leave the room and her masterful reply. "Yes, but don't take too long." She'd felt safe to speak up like this with Amanda sitting beside her like a security blanket. And she didn't want the students to think that Amanda was the only one who could be firm.

Claire smiled to herself and then said, "Nobody should be wandering around the school for an hour. It will look highly suspicious and you'd probably get reported to the principal. *I'm* talking about maybe spending ten minutes in the staff lunchroom to have a cup of coffee or happening to run into the janitor on the way there and chatting for a couple of minutes…brief interactions like that."

"Oh!" Gus said, deflated.

Amanda interjected at that point. You asked about anything unusual. I *did* see Nico's mother—that Angela woman—talking to Jessie's teacher in the hallway on the way down to the lunchroom. From the snatch of conversation I overheard, I gather that she was bawling the teacher out for not giving Angela the opportunity to meet Lydia before she was hired."

"So she's still on about that!" Claire muttered. "What a nasty wretch she is!"

Over the next few weeks, Gus and Amanda fell into a more or less regular routine. They attended to their lunchroom duties together three days a week, and then each of them had a day off. Of course, Gus, frequently managed to find a reason why she needed a second day off during the week, but Amanda didn't mind too much. After efficiently handling a few more incidents like the gum chewing one, she gained the respect of the students and was able to talk to them easily. More importantly, they were willing to talk to *her*.

It was in this way that she managed to find out a few items of possible use to their investigation. First of all, was the interesting tidbit she heard from several different students about Pamela Burton's apparent relationship with her husband, Gil. He'd turned up at the school on a few occasions either belligerently demanding some money from Pamela or accusing her of mismanaging some household task like not having ironed a shirt he wanted to wear. Apparently, Pamela never said anything back to him in her own defense and was clearly embarrassed by his tone. It was obvious that she always tried to get rid of him as soon as possible.

Second was the matter of the mysterious flowers that had arrived at the school for Pamela one day—a charming mixed bouquet of pink sweetheart roses, tiny white carnations and baby's breath—but with no card attached. This had led to various speculations by those who'd seen the flowers arrive.

Third, there was the matter of another older and more experienced classroom aide in the school who was sometimes asked to supervise Nico while Pamela attended to Jessie's exercises. This aide, named Bertha, had complained vociferously to others that if Pamela knew what she was doing, she'd be able to manage both of her charges quite easily and not be always pandering to Nico.

While students were confiding these types of remarks to Amanda, Gus was frequently wandering around the school. A large motivation for this was her boredom. Gus was often bored, as is the case for many people whose primary focus is themselves. But, in the course of her wanderings, Gus *did* find out some useful information on her own.

For instance, the school secretary, Doreen, told Gus that she'd overheard Pamela talking to the librarian, Georgette LeMoins, about a threatening phone call she'd received. The caller had told Pamela that something would happen to her if she didn't keep her mouth shut.

"Who was it and what did they say would happen?" Claire had asked Gus later that day.

"I don't know. That's all Doreen heard," Gus had replied.

Claire had not looked impressed and Gus vowed to herself that she'd find out more, and show Claire and Tia that she was a natural at this sleuthing business—on a par with them. The trouble was, Gus fumed, that they just lumped her in with Amanda. Well, Amanda was fine, but she really didn't have Gus' sleuthing instinct.

The next day, Amanda and Gus were at their school lunchroom supervision session together. Gus left shortly after the Junior High students arrived, in order to get serious about detecting. One little item she'd not yet shared with Claire and Tia was a student remark she'd overheard about some large basement lockers that the staff had available to them for any extra things they brought to the school, and how it was unfair that student lockers were so small in comparison.

Chapter 13: No Lock Too Strong

How am I going to find out if Pamela Burton, the dead assistant, had a locker and, if so, which one? And then, how would I get into it? Gus had asked herself, after she'd heard this remark. She'd thought then that Doreen, the school secretary, would be her best source and the best way to get her to share the information would be to give her a piece of information in return.

Gus wandered by the office that day and saw that Doreen was alone. She didn't seem that busy and was happy to engage in conversation. Gus told her jokingly what the student had said and implied that he was probably making it up. But Doreen disagreed.

"No, its true," she said. "See, the keys are all right there," and she pointed to a wall cabinet with the door hanging open and the keys neatly arranged and labeled by name inside.

"Aren't you supposed to keep the door locked? Anybody could just reach in and help themselves to a key."

"I don't lock it while I'm in the office. I can see right away if one of the staff is after a key, and I make sure they take the right one."

Gus had managed to casually walk by the cabinet without arousing Doreen's suspicions and get a closer look. It wasn't a very long look, though. Not good enough. She was able to catch Pamela's name on a key and the number *28* but nothing more. Gus went home that day feeling frustrated—but then she had an idea!

The next time Gus and Amanda were at the school together, Gus caught up with Lydia in the staff lunchroom and asked her if she had a locker. Lydia did. Gus then explained her plan to Lydia. Lydia was understandably doubtful. She was just starting a new job and not anxious to jeopardize it by getting involved in a sneaky act. She suggested that Gus just tell Inspector McCoy about the locker and let him take it from there. But Gus gave Lydia all the reasons why this wouldn't work and how they'd then lose their only chance to get into Pamela's locker. With deep reservations, Lydia finally agreed.

The next day, Lydia went to the office and asked Doreen for the key to her locker so she could get something out of it. Doreen handed her the key; Lydia thanked her and left and gave it to Gus. Gus had a copy made that afternoon and typed a label with Pamela Burton's name on it, matching the font and spacing as closely as possible to what was on the label of Lydia's key.

The next day was Thursday, the day Gus was supposed to have off, but she surprised Amanda by telling her she felt like going in with her that day. At lunchtime, she gave the newly created fake key to Lydia and asked her to swap it for the original.

Lydia walked into the office, apologizing profusely to Doreen for not returning her key the day before. "I'll just put it back," Lydia said, and moved briskly over to the key board, returned her key, covered her mouth with one hand as she faked a loud sneeze and leaned *involuntarily* against the board, where she quickly swapped the false Pamela Burton key for the real one. Doreen looked at her suspiciously and scanned the board to reassure herself that all the keys were there. Lydia said a quick good-bye and left, her knees quaking.

Gus was waiting for Lydia in the hall outside of view and Lydia handed the key to her silently and walked away. She did not look happy. Gus shrugged her shoulders and headed for the basement. She saw the tall lockers, all neatly numbered, as soon as she neared the bottom of the stairs. *Now if I just don't run into that janitor again,* Gus thought. She'd had an earlier confrontation with him on one of her previous ambles downstairs, the kind of leisurely strolling around the school as if it were her new domain that Claire had specifically advised against.

Gus recalled that exchange with Felix Merkel, the school janitor, all too well. She replayed it word for word now from her memory.

"Who are you and what are you doing wandering around down here?"

"I'm a new employee and I'm looking for my locker. My name is Augusta Kalline," Gus had blustered.

"You look kind of old to be a new employee. May I see some identification?"

"And who are you to be ordering me about?" Gus had responded, looking up and down at his dusty work clothes.

"I'm Felix Merkel, the building superintendent and I'm in charge of what goes on down here. Identification, please."

"I have not received my business cards yet. I'm in charge of the lunchroom," Gus said haughtily, not thinking it necessary to confuse the situation by mentioning Amanda's role.

"Oh. You're a temp, then. Well, temps are not allowed down here, so please leave. Otherwise, I'll call the principal," and he pulled out his cell phone.

"I'll speak to him myself about your rude behavior!" Gus said imperiously, and, mustering what dignity she could, she stomped up the stairs.

Chapter 14: The High Cost of Snooping

Gus looked furtively from side to side but nobody appeared to be in the dark basement hall where the lockers were located. She walked along tentatively until she found locker number 28. After another quick look over her shoulder, she opened the locker with no problem. *Almost too easy,* she thought.

The locker appeared to be empty except for a bottle of something on the upper shelf. Gus pulled it out and saw that it was half a 26 of modest Scotch whiskey— *Teacher's.* She put it back and stood there frustrated for a minute, but then she noticed a folded piece of paper wedged behind the shelf in the back corner. Gus was struggling to get it out when she felt strong hands on her back. In a moment, she was shoved into the locker and the door was slammed behind her. She heard the ominous click of a padlock and, only then, realized the full import of what had just happened.

Gus slowly and painfully managed to wiggle around in the tight space so that finally she was facing forward. She noticed the narrow bands of light coming through the locker vents and wondered if they'd allow enough air in. She began to pant in anticipation, but then forced herself to calm down. *What to do?*

Amanda would be getting anxious about her and what would she do? Maybe, she'd let the principal know and then they'd search the school. For a moment, Gus relaxed at that thought, but only for a moment.

Oh, no! If school personnel found her here, she'd have to explain how she got the locker key that she'd carefully placed in her pocket after opening the padlock. Then they'd find out about Lydia's involvement and that would be the end of Claire's grand plan. *Amanda will know what to do. She'll fix this somehow,* Gus thought, recognizing, in a moment of surprise, the steady wisdom of her friend and how much she had come to depend on it.

Gus huddled in the locker, unable to straighten up. Her shoulders and neck cramped and her knees ached. Periodically, she called out in an increasingly husky and weak voice, but nobody answered. She thought to herself, *maybe this is the end,* and wondered about all the things she'd not yet done in her life and had been planning to do. *What has my life meant anyway?* Gus asked herself. And the answer was not very comforting.

Meanwhile, in the lunchroom, Claire suddenly appeared in front of Amanda with Jessie in tow.

"What are you doing here?" Amanda stuttered.

"Lydia has a really bad headache. Maybe she's getting the flu after all the stress of the last week. Anyway, she can't cope any more today and Doreen called Nico's mother and me to pick up our kids early. Is Aunt Gus here today?"

"She wasn't supposed to be, but she came in with me anyway. She's wandering around somewhere, but I thought she'd be back by now," Amanda replied, a note of concern in her voice.

Just then, Jessie started to fuss and her arms flung rigidly into the air. Then both her arms and her legs started jerking spasmodically back and forth in a classic grand mal seizure. Amanda looked on in horror, but Claire turned away quickly and headed for the door. She decided to take Jessie to the empty part of the basement until the seizure subsided and Jessie recovered. There was no need to make a spectacle in front of everyone.

Claire found a quiet place in the middle of a row of lockers. She parked the wheelchair with the brakes on and attempted to adjust Jessie in her chair. Jessie was thrusting forwards so violently that she would have been on the floor except for her seatbelt. Then, as suddenly as it had begun, the thrusting stopped and Jessie slumped forward exhausted.

Chapter 15: Jessie to the Rescue

Claire walked Jessie in her chair back and forth along the basement corridor, as she could not transport her safely in the van in her limp state. After a few minutes, Jessie began to regain some tone and seemed to be coming back to her regular self. Claire was about to head for the elevator when she noticed the way Jessie had been tensing and orienting towards a particular bank of lockers every time they walked by them. It was not part of her normal post-seizure behavior and Claire paused to figure it out. Then she heard it, a faint scuffling sound and a hoarse whisper and it was coming from one of the lockers. *Could an animal have been trapped inside?* Claire asked herself. Well, it was not her problem, but she could tell Doreen, and Doreen could get someone to deal with it. She checked the locker number—28—and then started to move on, but Jessie howled.

Claire had always been proud of the fact that, despite all her problems, Jessie was good-natured. She and Dan were fond of saying that Jessie never complained without a good reason. Claire wheeled the chair over to the locker and said to Jessie, "What's wrong? What do you want?" There was no response from Jessie, but it was as if she were listening. Then Claire also heard something and it sounded eerily like her name. She waited and heard the faint scuffling sound again—and then something that sounded like *Jessie*, and Jessie made a noise in response.

Claire did not know what to make of this, but she moved closer to the locker and spoke directly into the slats, feeling a bit of a fool and hoping nobody would walk by. "Hello, is somebody there?"

"Claire," came a faint croak. "Help me!"

"Aunt Gus!" Claire responded in horror. "Is that *you?* How...."

"Claire, Claire, please! I can't hang on much longer."

"But the padlock is closed. I'll have to go to the office to get the key."

"No! Don't do that!" Gus responded in an agitated voice. "I *have* the key!"

"But how..."

"Here! I'll push it through the slat. Do you see it?"

"The slat isn't big enough. I better go for help."

"No, *no!* Then they'll know and Lydia will get in trouble."

At this point, Jessie started crying to add to the confusion. Claire searched desperately in her purse to find something to pry the slats apart with and finally settled on a nail clipper. She forced the clampdown part in until the pressure finally broke it off, but she had made some progress. Jessie stopped crying at this point as if she realized that something was happening. Claire managed to slide in the thin part of the clippers and finally wedged it in far enough that it started to raise the slat. Gus pushed the tip of the key out and Claire kept pushing until the slat moved enough for the key to fall through onto the floor outside the locker.

Claire quickly opened the padlock with trembling fingers and reached inside to help Gus out. She was too weak to stand up alone, but was able to hold onto the back of Jessie's chair. Claire was about to close the locker when Gus stopped her. "Wait! There's a scrap of paper wedged at the back of the shelf. Can you get it out? It may be a clue!"

Claire resisted at first, but Jessie started fussing again. She was feeling weak herself from the shock of it all, but with trembling fingers she finally managed to work the paper loose, close the door and lock the padlock. Just then, the school custodian came along.

"What's going on here? I heard noise!"

"Oh," Claire replied. "My daughter had a bad seizure and we brought her here to calm her down."

As if in response to this, Jessie started fussing again and Claire said, "We better take her home now." Gus had recovered enough by this point to walk, and she started pushing the chair slowly towards the elevator. The custodian looked at them quizzically, but said nothing.

"I wonder if he's the one who pushed me in," Gus muttered. "I had a run-in with him the other day when I was down here looking around."

"What? Never mind. I won't ask."

Gus was walking very slowly and it took a while to get to the van. Claire settled Gus in the front seat and then loaded Jessie in her chair into the back, grateful once more for the Swinger side lift that required less than three feet of space to load Jessie's chair, since another car had parked quite close despite the big sign in the window indicating wheelchair loading.

Jessie had settled down at this point and once Claire got in the car, she took a good look at Aunt Gus. Her face was white and she was trembling. Claire touched her hand and it was icy cold. "I'm taking you home with me, Aunt Gus, so I can look after you—unless you feel you need to go to the hospital to be checked out."

"I have no change of clothes or pajamas," Gus objected.

"I'll call Amanda to pack a bag for you, and Dan can pick it up later. Meanwhile, I want to get you home and into bed. I have a nightgown you can use. You don't look good at all. You need to lie down—and a cup of hot tea with lots of sugar should help."

"Claire, I want to explain," Gus said, and Claire noticed then that her lips had a bluish tinge.

"I don't care right now. I just want to get you home and into bed." Claire noticed that Jessie was being very quiet, as if she knew that Claire had all she could handle right now to look after Aunt Gus.

Later that evening, when both Jessie and Gus were sleeping soundly, Claire phoned Lydia and got the whole story. "I think she wanted to help and to impress you that she *could* help," Lydia said. "I didn't want to get involved, but she was very persuasive and I could see her point. There *might* have been something in that locker."

"We did find a scrap of paper, but I haven't even had a chance to look at it yet. I've been so worried about Aunt Gus. She looks so weak and frail. Just a minute; I'll get it now." Claire retrieved the paper and picked up the phone again. "I have it, Lydia, but it only has a few words and—it looks like—the beginning of a letter. I'm pretty sure it's in Pamela's handwriting, but I'll compare it later with her daybook entries for Jessie." Claire tried to read the paper, but it was very wrinkled. She ran to get a stronger light and then began to read. "'Dear Gil, I don't know how to say this bu...' And that's all there is. What do you think?"

"Hmm," Lydia responded. "It sounds like the beginning of a *Dear John* letter."

"Yes, it does. Maybe it was a draft she was working on and she stored it there to make sure nobody saw it. But if that's the case, who took the rest of it?"

"It could have been taken after she died. Maybe her husband was asked to empty out her locker. I could ask Doreen if anyone had thought to empty Pamela's locker."

"You'll have to find a way to return Pamela's key first before you talk to Doreen. Otherwise, she might grab the fake key to check it out for herself, and then she would know about the switch," Claire said. "I have the real key here and I can send it to you through Amanda."

Lydia agreed to wait to return the key and then to proceed cautiously. They ended the call and Claire went off to bed, suddenly realizing how exhausted she was after this latest adventure. Just before she drifted off to sleep, she chuckled to herself, visualizing her aunt slinking along the hall to find the locker. But then she remembered what a close call Aunt Gus had had and vowed to herself that they must all work doubly hard to find Pamela's killer before something worse happened.

Chapter 16: Claire Has a Brainstorm

The next day was Saturday and Claire didn't have to work and Jessie didn't need to go to school. Karen arrived at eight to look after her but, after Jessie was washed and dressed and had her breakfast, Aunt Gus just wanted to sit beside Jessie on the loveseat and keep her arm around her. *They really have formed a special bond these past couple of years,* Claire thought, *and it seems like Aunt Gus gets as much out of the relationship as Jessie—maybe more!*

"You and Dan go and relax now while I do the dishes," Karen ordered. I'll keep an eye on Jessie and start her program as soon as Aunt Gus is willing to part with her."

Claire and Dan retired to the sunroom to read the newspaper. But in a minute, Claire put the paper down to talk to Dan. She suddenly realized how shaky she still felt because of Gus's close call.

"I know Aunt Gus irritates you at times, Dan, but she was all I had after my mother died and my dad just withdrew into his work." Claire remembered those sad days, growing up with an unsympathetic stepmother. Gus wasn't the mothering type, but Claire always knew that in her own way, Gus really cared about her and missed her sister—Claire's mother—the way Claire did. Now that her father and step-mother were both gone, Aunt Gus was even more important to her. Claire had friends and she had Dan and Jessie, but they could not entirely replace her original family. Only Gus could do that.

Claire was still thinking about this after she'd gone back to reading the paper and had come to the travel section. Turning the page, she saw a big ad for sell-off vacations, an almost unbelievable deal for an all-inclusive week in the Bahamas at a 4-star resort. Suddenly, an idea flashed into her head and, as was usual for her, thought turned into action very quickly.

"Dan, you appear to be finished with all your road trips and conferences for awhile and I think it's time *I* took a vacation. And I want to take Aunt Gus with me. I think she needs to get away from everything after what happened yesterday."

"Well," Dan replied mildly. "First of all, my trips were *not* vacations. They were necessary for my work. But I grant you that the change of scene was nice. If you want to go, this would be a good time. Is Gus prepared to pay her way? She's pretty tight with her money."

"*I*'m going to pay for it," Claire said stubbornly. "I want her to know how much I care for her and that's a hard point to get across to Aunt Gus. But money she *always* understands. Paying for it will translate into caring in her mind, and right now I think she needs to feel cared for. She had a pretty bad scare yesterday."

"Have you any idea who did it?"

"No, and right now I don't care. I'm going to call Tia and see if she can cover for me at work and if she and Roscoe can help out Amanda at lunchtime. Then I'm going to call the travel company offering this deal."

"And when are you going to tell Gus?"

"After it's all settled and I have the tickets on hold. A deal like this is going to go fast." And with that, Claire got up and left the room to make her arrangements.

Tia was able to help out and Claire arranged for the two tickets. She was just putting down the phone when

Gus emerged from the family room where she'd finally agreed to turn Jessie over to Karen.

"Good morning, Aunt Gus. Did you sleep well? How are you feeling today?"

"Like a foolish old woman," Gus said mournfully. "Claire, I have to tell you what I did."

"No need, Aunt Gus. I called Lydia last night and she told me everything. Actually, I think it was a very clever plan. It just wasn't so smart going off on your own when there's clearly a murderer loose in the school! You looked terrible yesterday! I was afraid you were going to have a heart attack from the stress!"

"I was so scared, Claire. I've never been that scared in my life. I really thought it was the end. If it wasn't for Jessie...."

"Yes, that girl has definitely got good hearing—and some kind of sixth sense as well to make up for the other senses that are missing!"

"She recognized my voice, even though I could hardly talk at that point. I'm sure of it."

"You've formed quite a bond with her, Aunt Gus," Claire said gently.

"She kept reaching out and touching me when I was sitting beside her this morning, as if she knew I might not have been back."

"Well, you can see now why we could never give up on her."

"I understand that—now that I've gotten to know her. It takes time to really see who she is, doesn't it?"

Claire looked at her usually self-absorbed aunt in surprise and gratitude. "Yes, it does," she said softly with a catch in her voice. "Aunt Gus, I think we both need to get away for a while from all this nasty business. I've booked a trip for us to Grand Bahama Island for a week at a resort there."

"Oh, I could never afford that!" Gus exclaimed.

"Don't worry. It's all taken care of. It was a really good last minute deal. We leave Monday!"

"But..."

"I *do* earn a regular salary now, Aunt Gus, more than I ever earned with my part-time designer business."

"Just the two of us?" Gus said wistfully

"Just the two of us. We need to spend more time together without so many distractions all the time." Claire tried to decipher the look on Gus's face and decided that what she saw was what she'd been after. It was a look of renewed pride, of being important to somebody, of being loved and cared about, of counting—and Claire realized, sadly, how lonely and alienated Aunt Gus must have felt for much of her life. That look was worth twice the money she'd paid for the trip!

Chapter 17: With Claire a Holiday Is Never Just a Holiday

Unlike her previous exciting trip to Mexico, this trip to Freeport on the island of Grand Bahama was almost boringly smooth and brief, just five hours and 15 minutes direct from Edmonton. Aunt Gus blinked in amazement when she stepped out on the tarmac and looked around her, breathing in the tropical air. Claire realized suddenly that Aunt Gus was from a different generation and a different income bracket, a demographic that didn't take winter get-aways for granted—in fact, did not even consider them.

At the resort, they were assigned a modest room with two double beds, but in Aunt Gus's eyes it represented luxury. "Look!" she crowed. "Our own coffeepot and look at the balcony. We look right out on the ocean! And they gave us all those little bottles of shampoo and conditioner and lotion and even a shower cap and a little sewing kit. Do you suppose we could take them with us when we leave?"

"Many people do, Aunt Gus. I'm sure they wouldn't mind."

By the time they'd emptied their suitcases and arranged all their things, it was four in the afternoon Bahamian time, and Aunt Gus wanted to take a quick nap before supper.

"I'll just wander around for awhile," Claire said, "and find out where everything is. First, Claire made it a point to check the menus for the three special restaurants and find out where they were located. *Aunt*

Gus will enjoy those, she thought. Then she peeped out the front door to find out if there were any taxis regularly waiting there for when they wanted to go to the Port Lucaya market. But what she saw caused her to pull back in shock and move quickly out of the line of sight.

It can't be! she exclaimed to herself. *I came all this way to get away from her and the whole mess and there she is!* Claire was referring to Nico's mother who'd just stepped out of a taxi, accompanied by an annoyed-looking man who was presumably her husband.

"If you hadn't insisted on letting that man at the airport suck you into a tour of that other resort, we wouldn't have missed the bus!" Mr. Arietti scolded his wife.

"Yes, but we're getting a free guided tour of the island and all the highlights just for attending his spiel tomorrow morning," Angela responded.

The man had just finished paying the taxi driver and had a shocked look on his face. "$60 dollars American for a 15-minute ride! So you can write that off your freebie!" he exclaimed. "And by the time they finish with us, we'll have lost a day of our vacation. And don't even think about getting sucked into a timeshare because I won't sign!"

Angela looked embarrassed, aware that there were people around, and she walked quickly to the counter without replying to her husband. Claire quietly exited out the other door and headed briskly back to her room, her head swimming. Gus was awake and Claire related her sad tale. But Gus, with a few days rest since her ordeal and the excitement of the trip, had recovered her mojo.

"Look at the bright side!" Gus said. "Nico's mother doesn't know me. Maybe I can snoop around and hear some more of what they have to say to each other."

"Yes, Gus, but the other side of that is I'll have to stay hidden. Not my idea of enjoying my vacation!"

"Well, you said they talked about a tour. That day, at least, you'll be free to move around. When do you think it will happen?"

"Likely tomorrow morning," said Claire. "That's usually how those sharks set it up."

"Okay, then! Let's make the most of tomorrow and then I'll get busy snooping!"

It is clear that Aunt Gus has recovered, Claire thought sourly. *She's back to focusing on her plans and not worrying about anybody else!*

Two days later, Gus, wearing a large sun hat and glasses, spotted Angela Arietti and the man they assumed was her husband, settling down in twin chaise lounges by the pool. Gus wandered around and finally chose another unit next to them, but separated by a table. She placed a bored look on her face, turned her back on them and pretended to go to sleep with the beach towel judiciously draped over her lower body but exposing her arms and back for some sun—and the hat draped loosely over her head and face, presumably to keep the sun off. She lay very still, suffering the pangs of boredom that she was not good at tolerating. Finally, the Ariettis began to talk—at first in low voices but gradually louder.

"Do you really need another drink?" Gus heard him snarl.

"It's supposed to be a holiday. What do you want me to do? Sit here all day drinking water and waiting for the pearls of wisdom to drop from your mouth?"

"No. You've obviously made sure not to allow yourself to engage too deeply in anything *I* have to say. I recognize that semi-dazed expression. It's the same one I've seen and smelled many times when I come home from work—including when you were pregnant with Nico."

"Don't bring Nico up. He has some syndrome. It has nothing to do with alcohol!"

"Oh, yeah? Well, guess what? That's not what the doctors think!"

"What do you mean?" Angela asked suspiciously.

"That fancy new specialist you got, Dr. Wenzel? He called me at work the other day and asked me to visit him alone. I saw him the day before we left. He said you've consistently told every doctor you've seen about Nico that you didn't drink during your pregnancy. Yet they cannot find any sign of a syndrome or anything in Nico's birth history that would provide another reason for Nico's disabilities—and he has many of the characteristics of children with fetal alcohol spectrum disorder. "

"What characteristics? He's a beautiful child!"

"I thought so, too. But Dr. Wenzel pointed out that his eyes are a little close, the space above his upper lip is flattened, and his ears are low on his head. And his behavior problems all fit that profile as well. He has poor judgment, poor impulse control and no sense of the consequences of his actions. And you know that the school psychologist diagnosed him with attention deficit disorder."

"Yes! That's what it is! It runs in my family and it has nothing to do with alcohol! My father was a dreamer who could never stay focused on any one thing!"

"It's not the same, Angela. And you know it! Until you admit to the doctors that you drank almost every day of your pregnancy—and I know that's the case as much as you've tried to hide it from me—we can't help Nico. We've got to find a way to get his behavior under control. I've been reading up on kids with this syndrome and most of them end up in jail as adults. He has to learn that there are consequences and he cannot just do what he wants!"

"You're wrong!" she sobbed, and stormed off. A minute or two later, Gus heard Mr. Arietti following his wife. Gus got up painfully from her chair. It had been very hard to remain inert all that time and Gus knew she could not have tolerated it much longer. She limped back to their unit where she found Claire just completing a phone call home to check on Jessie.

Claire took one look at her and asked what had happened.

"It was in a good cause," Aunt Gus said grimly, and related what she'd heard, not hesitating to mention how heroic she'd been to remain still all that time even though she was in pain!

Yep. She's definitely back! Claire thought to herself. But she immediately forgave her aunt her bit of hubris because this was very valuable information.

"Wow, that's great information, Aunt Gus! I'm going to tell Gustaf! The school can require a recent diagnosis for Nico from a specialist in order to provide the best possible educational intervention. Once they have that, they can pass it on to the behavioral assessment unit that Lydia has been wanting to involve and maybe between them, they can make some progress with Nico—and create a more positive atmosphere for Jessie in the process!"

The rest of the week passed pleasantly enough, but with no further revelations. Their resort, Bayacar, had a sister unit next door and when Claire saw that Angela and her husband were spending most of their time lolling around the swimming pool at the home resort, Gus and Claire transferred their base of operations there. Every morning, Claire went off before breakfast, and Aunt Gus joined her at their prearranged meeting spot when she was ready. Together, they took tennis and archery lessons, sailed out on the catamaran and often just lounged on the beach in the afternoons for a couple of hours.

During those quiet times, they often talked and Claire learned many things about her aunt she hadn't known before, and now understood why she'd always felt such a strong sense of empathy coming from Gus when she was growing up. Gus had experienced even more neglect than Claire had in her childhood years— and, unlike Claire, she had not, as an adult, found a gentle, loving man who could help her to love herself and who could smooth her adjustment to the world around her. Clearly those early experiences had shaped who Aunt Gus was today.

They did not always talk of serious matters, though, and after spending some time perusing brochures, finally decided to take an island tour before returning home. Claire held her breath at pick-up time in front of the sister resort, worried that Angela and her husband would choose that day to take advantage of this very popular tour but it did not happen. They relaxed and enjoyed the various sights and especially the Garden of the Groves, a 12-acre park with thousands of different plants and many different birds and animals. There were even some little stores selling crafts and teas and healing salves made from a special native plant, and they particularly enjoyed the opportunity to interact with some of the local people. They learned a bit about island politics and history and the island way of life, an enriching addition to their so far rather insulated resort experience.

The tour had occurred on their last day and Claire dreaded the bus trip back to the airport—quite sure that she'd be discovered by Angela. But Aunt Gus pulled a rather flamboyant, orangey-red wig from her travel bag and an oversized pair of dark glasses. Angela looked at them suspiciously in passing, but said nothing and, apart from Claire having to tolerate an itchy head all the way home, they arrived back without the confrontation she'd feared.

Chapter 18: The School Takes Control

Principal Gustaf Lennon, was very interested in the information Claire reported to him, but, of course, he had no way of acting on it directly. A letter was sent to Nico's parents demanding a recent diagnosis, with the emphasis on *recent*. The explanation given was that the school was not able to provide an appropriate educational program for Nico based on the medical information they currently had on file for him.

With psychiatric *labeling* having recently become a hot potato issue, this request posed an ethical and legal minefield for Nico's pediatrician, and he was more than happy to hand the task over to Nico's most recent specialist. Thus, the school ultimately received a letter from a Dr. Wenzel that gingerly worked around the use of the term *fetal alcohol spectrum disorder* while at the same time saying that Nico demonstrated signs and symptoms "consistent with alcohol ingestion during early pregnancy" and since no other satisfactory explanation could be found for his particular pattern of disabilities, the school was advised that the most useful course of action would be to proceed with an intervention program similar to one that would be effective for individuals suffering from that syndrome.

In short order, the behavioral assessment team arranged a meeting with Nico's parents, his educational assistant and his teacher. Principal Lennon was sufficiently interested in Nico's case that he arranged to sit in as well, just to assure himself that the classroom teacher fully understood and accepted what was to happen. Up to this time, she'd been cowed into submission by Angela Arietti, but in a private meeting with her, Lennon had stated very firmly that that situation was not to go on.

Angela was angry and mortified by the working diagnosis presented during the meeting, based on the doctor's report—and the fact that her husband just sat there silent and stone-faced. Annick Bowen, the team psychologist, took the lead during the meeting and managed to create a warm, non-judgmental atmosphere and to get across the message that if they all worked together, there was a lot of hope for Nico's development.

Paolo Arietti, Nico's father, gradually opened up and asked a number of incisive questions about how to handle certain aspects of Nico's behavior. By the end of the meeting, he was looking happy and hopeful—a very different expression from the one he'd worn at the beginning of the meeting. However, Angela continued to look sullen and basically bored by the proceedings, shaking her head at every new suggestion and declaring in sneering tones that they'd already tried that and it didn't work. From time to time, Paolo looked at his wife and scowled. Annick Bowen said nothing, but made sure to ask for Paolo's work number before the meeting was over.

Although technically she was not allowed to do so, Lydia reported the key elements of the new behavior plan to Claire after the meeting, and Claire felt happy and hopeful for the first time about Jessie's new school placement. After the meeting, the classroom teacher seemed to have a new respect for Lydia because many of the ideas for modifying Nico's behavior that Lydia had been suggesting had been supported by the behavior team. She seemed to recognize that she was out of her league with Nico and left the management techniques for dealing with him increasingly to Lydia, agreeing that Lydia should just report to her on any changes.

It did not take long before Nico's behavior began to turn around, at least in some ways. He stopped running away—the most disturbing and labor-intensive element of managing his behavior. Why did this happen? Because he no longer got any form of attention from this act that could be considered remotely reinforcing. When he left, he was retrieved and wordlessly returned to the pullout room he shared with Jessie. He was never left alone, but was assigned seatwork while Lydia focused on meeting Jessie's needs. He was not scolded. There were no signs of exasperation on Lydia's part and it was as if the running away had never happened except for the sudden lack of direct attention. Lydia spoke to him in a calm voice only, correcting the seatwork if he did it and redirecting him if he did not. When he completed something right, she was quick to praise him and when he did not, she simply told him that she knew he could do better.

Of course, he escalated the negative behavior at first and the first two weeks were very draining. The principal saw this and reassigned Bertha to give Lydia some occasional relief. The intervention program was explained to Bertha in a private meeting, but it hardly needed to be. She understood intuitively what needed to be done and that had been the source of her previous frustration when Pamela had asked her to take over but clearly could not or would not deal effectively with Nico's negative behaviors or allow Bertha to try any different approaches other than the ones sanctioned by his mother Angela.

Together they—Lydia and Bertha—made it through those first very difficult two weeks, and it was then that they began to notice a shift in Nico's behavior. The additional surprise was that he now seemed happier and more content than previously. Annick Bowen had told them this was an expected outcome they frequently saw with behaviorally difficult children.

Chapter 19: Bad Karma or Just Bad Luck?

Claire was in the lunchroom one day with Roscoe, talking to Aunt Gus. Now that Nico's behavior was more manageable he was allowed to spend the lunch hour with the junior high students and Jessie was also there. Previously, she'd had to stay behind with Nico in their special pullout room for lunch except when Claire came with Roscoe to get her since Lydia or her lunch relief person, Bertha, could only be in one place at a time.

Claire was sporting a short bouncy wig since she'd had no time that morning to style her always difficult hair. She leaned towards Gus with her face in profile just as Angela Arietti entered the room.

"You!" Angela sputtered. *"You* were there! With *her!"* She pointed at Gus. "You were *spying* on me!"

"Quite the contrary!" Claire replied. "I went out of my way to avoid you. It was enough that seeing you there put a large dent in my holiday without returning the compliment!"

"Nonsense! And you wore that ridiculous wig on the plane just so I wouldn't recognize you! *Nobody* would wear a wig like that unless they were desperate to conceal their identity!"

"Humph," Gus could not help interjecting.

"And *you,* you old biddy! It was *you* that first day on the beach pretending to sleep so you could spy on us! I *knew* nobody on a noisy beach could lie that still that long if they were *really* asleep! And you told Claire what you think you heard me say. And *she* told the principal who got those behavior police involved—all on the basis of hearsay! I'm going to the school board about this to lodge a formal complaint. This isn't over!"

"Go right ahead!" Claire said, but with some loss of her usual oomph. It helped that Jessie started crying at that moment, obviously upset by the harsh voice. "I'm sure Mr. Lennon will tell you that the timing was just a coincidence. They'd been considering involving the team for awhile." As soon as the words were out of her mouth, Claire knew she'd made a mistake. But it was too late to take them back.

"*What?* He's been talking to you about *my son?* Breach of confidentiality! Unprofessional behavior! I'll have his *job* for this!"

"*This* is unprofessional behavior—talking like this in front of *students!*" and Claire noted that the students were all listening avidly. "I'm *leaving!* We can resume this conversation when you're in a more balanced mood." Claire looked at her aunt, but carefully avoided addressing her as such.

"I'm leaving, *too,*" Gus added. "I've never been so disgusted in my *life!* You sound like a *fishwife!*" She quickly gathered her things and, with only a quick fleeting glance at Amanda who nodded her head, she flounced out of the room behind Claire.

They reached the van together, Gus walking faster than her usual speed, fueled by nerves. But then it took some time for Roscoe to climb awkwardly into the back and fasten the unfamiliar seatbelt. Finally, they were on the road.

"Why that lady *talk* like that, Claih? She not *nice* to you!"

"It's okay, Roscoe. Don't worry about it. She has some problems."

When they got back to Roscoe's home, Claire set him up with math homework in his room and told him that when it was done—and *only* when it was done—he could play his computer game for awhile. She also said she wanted to talk to Gus alone and he needed to stay in his room so they could talk privately.

Roscoe agreed soberly and once again Claire reflected on what a nice, considerate person he was! Then she put the kettle on, phoned Tia and asked her to come over, saying it was urgent. Only then did she sit down. She suddenly realized her hands were shaking. "Why me?" she asked Gus. "I never get away with *anything!* I must have bad karma!"

Gus said nothing but only shook her head mournfully. "I thought I did a good job of pretending to sleep at the resort! How did she *know?"*

Tia arrived then carrying half an apple cake, already warmed up. Claire grabbed some plates and forks and rapidly ate two pieces. "I see you're *really* upset," Tia said drily. Unfortunately, food was the go to comfort place for Claire in times of stress, and that did much to explain the 20 extra pounds she was carrying and never managed to lose.

While Claire was focusing in on the cake, Gus gave a fairly accurate summary of the recent confrontation with a perhaps unnecessary emphasis on the wig insult. But Claire just let her talk, moaning occasionally and muttering to herself between bites.

"Woah!" was all Tia could manage to say when Gus had finished telling the tale. "What are you going to *do,* Claire?"

"I don't *know* what to do—and right now I can't even *think* straight. That's the reason I called you over. I thought maybe you might have a suggestion!"

"Well, I think the first thing you should do is talk to the principal, preferably before *that woman* gets to him."

"It might already be too late for that," Claire moaned.

"Look, it's just your word against hers, and from what you've said, she's already presented herself as irrational and difficult to deal with."

"But that hardly justifies *spying*. And the worst thing is what I blurted out about the principal considering involving the behavior management people previously. *He* didn't tell me that. Lydia did—and it won't take him long to figure out that that's where it came from, especially since Angela's going to have him under the gun with the school board. Lydia could lose her job and *then* where will Jessie be!"

They talked further, but nobody had any better suggestions and soon Roscoe came out of his room with his completed homework sheet and the meeting broke up.

Chapter 20: The Day of Reckoning

The feared call to meet with the principal arrived the following Monday and the meeting was set for Wednesday. Lydia was there looking pale and frightened; Angela was there looking angry and self-justified; and Claire's own presentation was very subdued. The classroom teacher and the principal were also present. A Mr. Thomas Abbott was there representing the school board, and the principal deferred to him to run the meeting.

"Ms. Angela Arietti has lodged a formal complaint against Ms. Claire Burke, Ms. Alana Proux, Ms. Lydia Crestwell and Mr. Gustaf Lennon. She alleges: that she is being persecuted by Ms. Burke who even followed her to the Bahamas to spy on her during a recent holiday. She further states that one of the new lunchroom attendants—Ms. Augusta Kalline—was part of this conspiracy and did the actual spying on Ms. Arietti during her vacation, while Ms. Burke deliberately remained hidden to avoid detection."

Claire started to speak, but Thomas Abbott put up his hand to stop her.

"Ms. Arietti has also stated that confidential information about her son's program needs and the strategies being explored by the school to assist him was given to Ms. Burke by one or more of the following: Alana Proux, Lydia Crestwell and/or Gustaf Lennon.

"She has suggested that Ms. Burke negotiated the hire of her aunt, Ms. Augusta Kalline, and her friend,

Ms. Amanda Roche, to spy on her and her son at school, and that the school did not go through the proper procedures to hire these two women as lunchroom attendants. Furthermore, she argues that the only reason the hiring of these two women was necessary in the first place is that Ms. Burke maneuvered her daughter's personal assistant into the position of classroom aide with the collusion of Mr. Lennon and Ms. Proux."

"It wasn't like that..." Alana Proux sputtered.

"Please wait until I am finished, Ms. Proux."

Ms. Arietti further claims that the reason for maneuvering the hire of Ms. Lydia Crestwell was so that Ms. Burke could exert undue influence over the running of the school program for Nico and Jessica, ensuring that her daughter's needs were met first at the expense of those of Ms. Arietti's son.

Ms. Arietti states that the situation has become unworkable and the only reasonable solution is for Jessica to leave the school since Nico was here first. Lydia Crestwell, who is the most likely source of the leak, according to Ms. Arietti, should also leave the school. She is claiming that Ms. Crestwell is biased because of her pre-existing relationship with Ms. Burke. Another assistant can then be hired for Nico, and Ms. Arietti mentions that she has somebody appropriate whose name she would like to put forward."

"But Nico..." Lydia started to say, but Thomas Abbott held up his hand again.

"The claims are laid out in this statement that I'm passing around. I will give each of you a chance to respond to them and I would appreciate it if you would do so in the order in which they are laid out to avoid confusion and unnecessary redundancy. Ms. Burke, would you like to begin?"

"Yes," Claire said, clearing her throat while she quickly reviewed the paper. "I'd like to start by laying one of these matters to rest immediately. I had no idea that the Ariettis had booked the same tour when I booked the holiday for my aunt and myself. As for avoiding them, that part is true. I have found Ms. Arietti very difficult and unpleasant to deal with...."

At this point, Angela tried to interject but Thomas Abbott held up his hand firmly.

"As I started to say, she's hard to deal with. This was a much needed holiday for my aunt and myself and I didn't want to sour it by risking a confrontation." It is also true that my aunt accidentally overheard a rather disturbing discussion between Ms. Arietti and her husband and told me the details, but I certainly didn't ask her to listen to this conversation." In this manner, Claire managed to skirt around the issue of whether she'd hoped that Aunt Gus would overhear *any* conversation.

Claire consulted her paper and carried on. "As for the business of involving the behavior management unit to deal with Nico's, at times, very disruptive behaviors..."

Angela started to stand up in outrage but Thomas Abbott waved her back into her seat.

Claire continued. "*I* am actually the one who suggested to Nico's and Jessica's former assistant, Pamela Burton, that they be called in. I had this conversation with her some time in the first month of the school year when it was clear that Nico's behaviors were making it impossible for Jessica to have the program she needed and deserved

"After my Aunt Gus reported to me the conversation she overheard from the Ariettis—and I won't mention the details here——I was all the more convinced that only the behavior management team could provide a solution to Nico's behavior problems that, quite apart from what they were doing to undermine his academic development, were seriously undermining my daughter's quality of life. I *did* report this conversation to the principal—and, I might mention, that *I* am not bound by any rules of confidentiality. What he chose to do with that information, I have no direct knowledge of. However, I could not help but notice the sudden presence of a representative from the behavior management team in Nico's and Jessica's shared pullout room one day recently when I dropped by."

"I will deal with the next two points together," Claire continued. "After the tragic death of Pamela Burton, one of my first thoughts was who would replace her? Contrary to what Ms. Arietti believes, it's far more difficult to find and train somebody to meet Jessie's special needs than those of her son who, after all, can at least walk and talk and tie his shoelaces. I thought right away of Lydia Crestwell because not only could she start in immediately as she was thoroughly familiar with dealing with Jessie, but I also knew she had some background in dealing with individuals like Nico with behavior management issues."

Angela started to object to this characterization of Nico, but Thomas Abbott quickly stopped her.

Claire went on. "I don't know how Ms. Arietti spends her days, but I now work full-time and I could not just put my life on hold for two or three weeks while the school found and trained somebody else. Anyway, Lydia was interested in taking the job and the school checked her credentials and found them satisfactory, so they hired her. I had nothing more to do with that. All *I* did was ask her if she'd consider applying for the position.

"I then needed to find somebody to replace Lydia to provide some part-time care for Jessie at my home. I had noticed the way Karen, the lunchroom supervisor operated and I was impressed. I asked her if she'd be interested in such a position and she was. However, to her credit, she didn't want to leave the school in a bind and that's when I thought of asking my aunt and her friend, Ms. Roche, to take over the lunch hour supervision jointly. This way, I thought, it would not be too hard on these two retired ladies."

Claire could see that the principal was a little agitated at this point and obviously wanted to say something. She guessed what it was. "I should add that when I asked the principal if he was willing to arrange an interview with these two ladies for the position, he did tell me at the time that it was particularly difficult to fill the lunch hour supervision role. Few people were willing to break up their day like that for the minimum wage provided, all that the school could afford." Claire saw that Mr. Lennon had relaxed back in his seat and knew that she'd guessed correctly. "In any case, it appears to have worked out satisfactorily." At this, the principal nodded his head and Claire was silently grateful that nobody had found out about the locker debacle.

"Next, I'd like to address the claim that Lydia *told* me about the behavior management team coming in. She did *not.*" Here Claire was on shaky ground, but she was pretty sure there was no direct evidence to the contrary. "As a matter of fact, Lydia has been so busy with her new job that I've had very little contact with her except for the discussions on Jessica's progress I see in her daybook. I've brought the book with me for you to inspect. I don't think you'll find any reference to Nico in it, just as I hope that there would be no reference to Jessica in Nico's daybook." Claire reached over and handed the book to Thomas Abbott.

"Finally, on the matter of Jessie leaving the school, I would not agree with that and would, in fact, file a grievance with the school board and if that didn't work, to the minister of education. *You* chose to put her here," and with this Claire made a sweeping gesture to all the educational personnel in the room, "and it has been a very difficult adjustment for Jessie and our family. She lost a lot being jerked out of her elementary school setting and I'll not sit back and tolerate another move without a fight!" Claire sat back in her chair and clasped her hands together in front of her stomach to keep them from shaking. "I believe I have now responded to all the claims being made against me so that's all I have to say at present. Thank you for listening."

The room was silent, a sign that Claire's statement had made an impact. She had presented her actions as reasonable and appropriate, and the onus was clearly back on Angela Arietti to prove otherwise. After a moment, Mr. Abbott thanked her and then asked Mr. Lennon if he had anything to add.

"No," he replied. "I believe Ms. Burke has presented the situation correctly as I understand it."

"Ms. Crestwell, would you like to comment?"

"I just want to say that it's quite true what Claire says about how busy I've been. I have certainly had no time for gossip. I also want you all to know that I'm concerned about providing the best intervention possible for both Nico and Jessica. And the involvement of the Behavior Management Team has certainly helped with Nico. I've seen some very exciting gains with him recently. He's not running out of the room nearly as much!" Lydia sat back in her chair breathing heavily. It was quite obvious that she found this whole process highly intimidating.

"Thank you," Mr. Abbott acknowledged. "Ms. Proux?"

"Mr. Lennon and I made the decision to hire Lydia based on the fact that her qualifications, her full knowledge of Jessie's program and her immediate availability met our need, and our decision had nothing to do with the fact that she knew Ms. Burke—and I've found her work to be very satisfactory. I'd also like to add that the previous assistant Pamela Burton actually talked to me about involving the Behavior Management Team early in October, but when I discussed it with Ms. Arietti, she objected, believing it was unnecessary and would only upset Nico."

"Thank you, Ms. Proux. Well, I believe we've now heard from all the interested parties involved in defending against these claims. Ms. Arietti, is there anything you'd like to add at this point?"

Angela spent several minutes attempting to discount pretty well every statement Claire had made, but when it became clear that she was beginning to repeat herself, Thomas Abbott drew the meeting to a close. The entire meeting had been taped and he explained that the tape would be reviewed and a decision rendered as to the merit of the claims being made and any follow-up action required within the next week.

Chapter 21: One Step Forward; Two Steps Back

It had been a morning meeting and Claire went directly to Tia's house when it was over. She'd arranged for one of the other assistants at Roscoe's home to cover for her that morning, and she was in no state of mind to jump right back into her duties.

"How did it go?" Tia asked anxiously. She noticed that Claire was literally vibrating.

"Oh, I'm *so* glad that it's over! I was so tense at the beginning I thought I was going to be sick. But Mr. Abbott from the school board had all of Angela's claims listed on a two-page handout and when I started talking, I just followed the handout and that made it easier."

"Angela didn't have that advantage when she tried to rebut my statements, and she ended up rambling and repeating herself. I think she lost some credibility in the process. And if I'm any judge of body language, I think that Mr. Abbott saw me as being frank and truthful. Now I need a drink and a couple of pieces of your apple cake to celebrate that it's over!"

Tia looked at Claire thoughtfully and said, "Go sit down in the living room in Jimmy's recliner. I'll put on some relaxing music and be right back to you. Claire did as she was told and gradually her heart rate slowed. The more she thought of it, the more she was beginning to believe that she'd done well in countering Angela's claims and that the remarks from the others had only corroborated what she'd said. She was suddenly very tired and quite hungry—it *was* almost lunchtime—but her stomach felt squeamish.

When Tia returned with her offerings, Claire was dozing lightly and she opened her eyes in surprise. She was even more surprised when she saw what Tia had brought her. Instead of the cake she was expecting and, hopefully, a glass of wine, Tia presented her with a bowl of homemade vegetable soup, a lightly buttered multi-grain bun and a cup of ginger tea.

Claire raised her eyebrows and Tia said defensively, "Look, Claire, you always try too hard at everything and get all worked up. Then, after, you seem to think that the only way you can relax is to eat sweet stuff or drink...or both. It's not healthy and not necessary—it's just a bad habit. You already have some high blood pressure issues and I've noticed that you've put on some weight since I met you. I care about you a lot and I don't want to contribute to any health problems down the road for you."

Claire felt a confusing mix of emotions: hurt, embarrassment—and a surprising sense of gratitude. She was not used to people caring about her. Her stepmother certainly hadn't and her father had always been focused on his work and rather remote. She'd felt some affection from Aunt Gus, but only during her sporadic and infrequent visits. She knew that Dan cared about her, as she did about him, but they were usually so preoccupied with the conflicting demands of work and meeting Jessie's many needs that there was little time to show it. The steady support and affection she'd felt from Tia meant a lot to her and Tia's opinion of her was therefore very important.

Claire said nothing in response to Tia's statement. She didn't know what to say. Instead, she ate her soup and bun and was surprised that it seemed to settle her stomach and have a soothing effect. After that, they sat together companionably, drinking their ginger tea. Claire then shared the document that Mr. Abbott had handed out, and gave Tia a point-by-point replay of how she'd rebutted the various points. She could see that Tia was impressed and hopeful about how the meeting had gone.

The following Friday, Claire arrived home from work to find a letter addressed to her from the school board and labeled *personal and confidential*. Her heart pounded as she opened it, expecting the worst, but she was surprised and relieved by what she found. Ms. Arietti's claims were not sufficiently substantiated to warrant pursuing the matter further, but all parties involved were urged to remain vigilant in protecting the confidentiality of both Nico and Jessie. And Claire was specifically requested not to pass on any more undocumented information to school board officials. *I can live with that*, Claire thought, and happily phoned Tia to tell her the good news.

Chapter 22: More Bad Karma

Claire's relief was short lived, however. The following Monday, at eleven in the morning, she received a call from the school on her cell phone.

"Hello, Claire. This is Doreen from the school office. I'm phoning to let you know that Lydia has had an accident and the ambulance is on its way. We need you to come to the school and pick up Jessica. Bertha has Nico and her in the pullout room."

"What happened? How badly is Lydia hurt?"

"I'm not allowed to talk about it, Claire. Please just come as quickly as you can!"

Claire ended the call and then called Tia, explaining to her what little she knew. "I'll stay with Roscoe," Tia said. "You get Jessie and bring her back to the house. Can you manage with her here? I'll stay and help."

"Yes. I can grab some of the extra supplies from the school to get us through the day and return them later."

"Good! And don't forget to snoop around while you're there and find out what happened to Lydia."

"I intend to!" said Claire as she whipped out the door.

But Claire was met with a wall of silence at the school, and she had to wait until she was able to talk to Lydia that evening to find out what had actually happened. Obviously, the school board letter had had an impact on the principal, too, and he must have interpreted the confidentiality requirement to apply to everyone in the school—not just the students. Or maybe the school board lawyer was advising silence because of possible liability issues.

Lydia was still groggy with painkillers when Claire visited her in the hospital that evening, and by the look of her bandaged face and wired chin, Claire could see that Lydia was not going to be able to tell her what had happened. Claire whipped a pen and paper out of her purse and raised her eyebrows at Lydia, not wanting to alert the nurse busying herself nearby to what she was asking.

Lydia wrote the following with some difficulty. "I opened microwave to warm Jessie's snack. Microwave fell out, hit my face and broke my jaw—two teeth too. Knocked me to ground and fell on my stomach. There is some internal bleeding. Don't know...." Lydia stopped writing and turned to the wall, crying softly.

"Oh, no!" was all Claire could say. She spent the next few minutes just quietly rubbing Lydia's back and occasionally patting her hair. Finally, she said, "What can I do, Lydia? Is there anything at all? Just say the word and I'll do it."

Lydia wrote, "My parents. They are travelling. My sister knows—ph. 780-9368071."

Claire read the message silently.

Lydia reached back for it painfully. Then she wrote in a scrawling hand, "I want my mom!" She turned to the wall again and started crying with necessarily muffled sobs. A nurse came over and shooed Claire away but Claire managed to grab the paper before she left.

Once she was home, Claire made the call. "Hello," she said, when the phone was picked up. "Are you Lydia Crestwell's sister?"

"Ye-e-s. Who's calling, please?"

Claire introduced herself and explained what had happened to Lydia. Her sister, Celia Johnson, was angry and upset. "Why wasn't I notified?" she asked in a tight voice.

"Were you listed as next of kin? That would be all the information the school had to go on…whatever was in her wallet or in her personnel file at school. I only found out about you when I visited Lydia in the hospital this evening and she gave me your number. Can you get in touch with your parents?"

"I can try. They're driving across the country to visit relatives in Toronto. Maybe they phoned my aunt when they stopped tonight and she knows where they're at."

"Well, please try. Lydia is in the post-surgery unit at the Royal Alec hospital. She's really banged up and she wants her mom."

"I'll do everything I can to get hold of them. Unfortunately, they're not into social media or email or even cell phones. I *told* them they'd be sorry one day! One way or another, I'll visit Lydia in the morning and try to talk to her doctors."

"We've become very close," Claire said. "I'd really be grateful if you would share whatever you find out. This should not have happened. I find it hard to believe it was an accident."

"What do you mean?"

Claire hesitated for a moment, but then decided that Celia had a right to know and she told her what had happened to Pamela Burton.

Celia was predictably horrified and her first thought was that Lydia should not return to the school and that she was going to do her best to convince her to quit.

Me and my big mouth! Claire thought sourly.

Chapter 23: Claire Has To Know

That evening, Claire and Dan talked about the care situation for Jessie. It was not at all clear if or when Lydia would be coming back.

"Dan, I need you to take over with Jessie tomorrow morning so I can go to the school and find out what's happening. I'm pretty sure Angela will be using this opportunity to insert her desired candidate into the situation. But I also want to know if what happened to Lydia was really an accident. I actually used that microwave once when I was visiting Jessie in her pullout room. It seemed pretty securely in place to me!"

"Okay, I can take the day off, Claire, and do whatever work I must do from home on the computer. But just be careful, please!"

"I will, Dan—and thanks." Claire realized she should not have to thank him for looking after his own daughter, but somehow, in the ever-stranger North American dance between the sexes this was still seen by many women as the appropriate response.

Dan turned to Jessie and outlined to her their plans for the day. She half-gurgled and half-giggled her own special, slack-mouthed sound of happiness that she was going to have her favorite person all to herself. And Claire had the definite sense that Jessie was willing Claire to leave soon!

At the school the next day, Claire marched directly to the principal's office, tapped gently on the door that was partially open and stuck her head in when she saw he was alone and not on the phone.

"Oh, hello, Claire," he said wearily and with a marked lack of enthusiasm. "What can I do for you?"

"Hello, Gustaf. You look very tired." At earlier meetings, he'd asked her to call him by his first name and, although the latest debacle had put a damper on their relationship, Claire decided that she needed to try her best to retrieve that earlier level of connection if she was to make any progress.

He did not answer her directly but asked if she'd seen Lydia.

"Last night in the hospital," she said simply. "Lydia gave me her sister's number. She wants her parents to know what happened and they're travelling right now to visit relatives across the country. Lydia's hoping her sister can track them down."

"Did you give that information to the hospital?" Gustaf asked a bit sharply.

"No, I wasn't sure if she wanted them to know. If the hospital or the police want that information, they can always ask her like I did. All they need is a paper and pen for her to write the answer since she can't talk right now. You probably know that her jaw was broken and is wired shut." Claire said all this with a certain coolness in her tone and Gustaf got the message.

"Look, Claire, we're both still upset over Angela Arietti's accusations and are probably both wondering what, if anything, we did wrong. I know I am anyway. I've always found you pleasant and reasonable to work with and the program adjustments you've required for Jessie make sense and seem to be working for her. Therefore, your goals for her as your daughter and our goals for her as a student in our school are in sync. It follows from that, that we should have a harmonious working relationship. However, that is not the case with all the parents we work with in our school, including many whose children have no recognizable disabilities.

"We believe we should be able to work closely and openly with you on any matters pertaining to your child while at the same time respecting the confidentiality of any other child in our school, so you can see how special difficulties arise when two children are as closely interconnected in their educational programs as Nico and Jessie, and why we have to be extra careful in situations like this to be fair and respectful to all concerned."

This was the longest speech Claire had ever heard Gustaf make and it sounded somewhat pompous and a little rehearsed. She imagined that he'd received a private refresher course from Thomas Abbott and had extracted some of his phraseology from whatever discussions on the matter that had taken place between them.

"I'll keep that in mind," Claire responded, "and try my best to maintain proper boundaries. And I want you to know that I really appreciate how supportive and accommodating the school has been in meeting Jessie's needs since Lydia has been here."

Gustaf smiled and seemed to relax a little, looking more like his former self—the self it had been so easy and comfortable to talk to. Claire took the opportunity to cautiously proceed with the main point of her visit. "Lydia may not return to the school. I don't know. She's had a bad shock and a serious injury. Her sister, for one, is up in arms about it and plans to do her best to convince Lydia to leave. I think we can agree that Lydia was making excellent progress with both Jessie and Nico and it would be a shame to lose her and risk going back to how things were before?"

Gustaf said nothing and Claire added with a slight note of acerbity in her voice. "You can just nod your head if you agree. That way you won't risk speaking out of turn."

Gustaf rolled his eyes, refusing to play such a ridiculous game. "Of course, I agree," he said resignedly.

Claire said more cautiously, "Angela made it quite clear in the meeting that she wants to bring in a new *person* she's found whom she considers appropriate for dealing with Nico. I won't ask you to comment on that. I just want you to be aware of my position. I'll strenuously fight a return to the untenable situation we had before. And if the school has to rehire, I'd like to have a member of the behavior management team sitting in on the interviews to assess the candidates for their appropriate job skills for this position, both in terms of meeting Jessie's needs as well as Nico's needs. That's all I have to say on the subject. I plan to continue visiting with Lydia, but I'll try very hard not to put any pressure on her to return. It has to be *her* decision."

Gustaf nodded his head and this time he risked speaking briefly. "I understand and respect your position." He stood up thinking the interview was over.

Heartened by this, Claire hastily added, "There's one other thing you should know. A couple of weeks ago, I visited Jessie in the pullout room. I was very tired that day and I asked Lydia if I could warm a cup of water in the microwave to make some tea. I always carry a few bags in my purse. When I opened the microwave and pulled my cup out, it seemed rock solid to me and I was not being gentle. I can't help thinking something happened to it since, and that leads me to wonder if the microwave being unstable enough to fall on Lydia like that was really an accident."

Gustaf looked at her in surprise but said nothing.

Claire was becoming more and more annoyed by his new, mealy-mouthed approach and asked, "Don't you think you should ask the police to examine the microwave and surrounding area carefully and tell them about my experience?"

Gustaf hesitated for a moment, obviously inclining towards caution. Claire raised her eyebrows in irritation, a faint note of disgust in her face. Whatever else Gustaf was, he was a sensitive man and basically a fair man. Finally, he responded, "A representative from the Health and Safety Board has already contacted me. He'll be coming in to assess the situation for himself. If he decides to contact the police based on his examination, that will be up to him. I can't really tell him how to do his job." As an afterthought, he added in a low voice as if he were speaking to himself, "And if that happens, there may be liability issues involved."

Claire nodded in response. "I understand," she said simply, a depth of meaning behind those two words. She smiled, said her good-byes and left.

Chapter 24: The 'Accident' Investigation Begins

As Claire pulled out of the parking lot, Angela was pulling in, and she glared at Claire. *What was all that about?* Claire wondered. *Ahh! She probably thinks I got to Gustaf before her. And she's right!*

Claire drove home wondering what was going to happen. She decided that she better check on Lydia and called the hospital to see if visitors were allowed for her during the afternoon.

"Yes," the desk clerk replied, after consulting her papers.

Lydia was looking anxious when Claire arrived. She'd been given a notebook and pen, and wrote quickly, "What's happening at school? Did they find someone to take my place?"

"I just saw the principal, Lydia. He didn't even talk about that. He's preoccupied with the upcoming visit from the Occupational Health and Safety people. He's worried the school will be held accountable for this 'accident'."

"*Was* it an accident, Claire? I've been lying here thinking," Lydia wrote. "I used that microwave a lot of times, and it never seemed loose to me."

"I only used it once," Claire responded. "I don't remember noticing anything funny about it." After a pause, she added, "I think I need to get into that room and see for myself what happened. Do you think I could convince Doreen to let me in?"

Lydia penned a long answer that took her several minutes to complete. Her forearms and wrists were also badly bruised as she'd instinctively thrown up her hands to protect herself when the microwave had fallen. "I don't know—but what I *do* know is something funny is going on in that school and I don't want to go back to work there until we find out what. Do you think the school board would let you home school Jessie and let me work with her at your house?"

"I doubt it—and even if they did, it would only be for a half day and only after months of assessment and program planning."

"Well, what are you going to *do,* then?"

Claire thought a minute and then said, with more determination than she felt, "I'm going back to the school and find a way to get into that room."

Claire checked her watch and left soon after. It was now 2:15, so there was not much time. She planned her strategy. When she got to the school, she went directly to the room and memorized the number of Nico's and Jessie's pullout room. Although she'd been there many times, Claire had never really noticed the room number. In fact, she'd never even noticed that there was a number. Every time she went there, Claire was totally goal-focused—her usual state. Hence, she didn't notice things that had no direct bearing on her immediate future plans. This was not the first time that her habit of single-mindedness had brought her grief.

"It's 3-6G. What a pointless number!" Claire muttered to herself as she quickly hustled towards the office, Doreen and her collection of keys. She contemplated what she'd say to Doreen but nothing came to mind.

In the office, Claire looked at Doreen, and Doreen looked at Claire as she rushed in. *Something unspoken passed between them*, Claire thought. "I need the key!" Claire blurted out. "I'll have it back in fifteen minutes!"

"Sorry, I can't help you right now," Doreen replied. "Please excuse me. I need to use the washroom urgently. Bad clams!" Doreen left her desk hastily without looking back. Claire grabbed the key after looking over her shoulder, and raced off to the pullout room. Classes were in session and nobody was in the hallway. She entered the room quickly, but didn't dare turn on the light. Just then, her phone buzzed, causing Claire to jump. She quickly turned it off, hoping nobody next door had heard the sound. Then Claire raised the blinds slightly and squinted at the microwave. A stray ray of sunlight glinted off something beneath it. She raised the blind higher and went to examine the microwave close up. She ran her hands beneath it and they emerged greasy. *If this grease is run-off from food, then everybody who used this microwave recently is in danger of radiation poisoning!* was her first thought.

Claire explored beneath the microwave more thoroughly. *A lot of grease and all the way to the back!* She held her fingers to her nose. There was no smell of stale cooking grease. If anything, it smelled like fresh vegetable oil. Claire grabbed a couple of napkins to cover her hands and then gently moved the microwave back and forth. Somebody had obviously put it back in its place after the accident, but it moved very easily—slid—really. Careful not to pull it off, Claire turned the microwave slowly to one side. She could see from the kinks in the cord that it had once been tied up tightly to create a short cord, but that was no longer the case. *Interesting*! she thought, but just then she heard voices outside the door.

Chapter 25: A Close Call

"This is the room. We've kept it locked since the incident." Claire recognized Gustaf's voice and was grateful she'd pushed in the lock button on the door when she'd entered as she heard fumbling, scraping noises with a key. Gustaf was obviously using his master key that didn't work as quickly as the individual room keys. *What should I do?* Claire asked herself, panicking momentarily. But then she remembered the craft closet, quickly entered it, and closed the door behind her.

Soon, however, Claire's curiosity got the best of her and she opened the door slightly to hear what was being said.

"There's a lot of oil or grease under this microwave. Was somebody trying to cook French fries in it?"

"Oh, no, Mr. Lund!" Gustaf responded. "It was strictly used to warm up meals for the two students who used it and, perhaps occasionally, by their assistant heating up her lunch."

Mr. Lund, obviously from the Occupational Health and Safety Board, moved the microwave gently back and forth. Then he repositioned it, took out a level and placed it diagonally across the top. After writing something in his notebook he turned the microwave around and observed the kinks in the unfastened cable just as Claire had done. He examined the front of the shelf and took out a ruler from the kit he was carrying. He measured the distance between two small holes spaced about six inches apart and a line of lighter paint

8-inches long and ½ an inch wide across the front of the shelf. Then he turned soberly to Gustaf. "The shelf slopes down from back to front about five degrees. Someone nailed a small board here in front at some point, presumably to keep the microwave secure. That was also the likely reason the cord was tied up tight behind as an extra precaution—as you can note from the kinks in it. When was the last time you remember seeing this board here?"

"I never come in here," Gustaf faltered. "You'd have to ask Lydia. Maybe *she* knows."

"Lydia?"

"The assistant—but she's only been here a few weeks. She's the one who was hit by the microwave. But she's still in the hospital."

"That makes it difficult. But in any case, I think you should get the police involved. Something is off here— and *they* will be able to talk to her."

"No-o-o. Is that really necessary? The school—"

"Well, there *is* one more thing I can check first—the source of that oil or grease under the microwave." Lund looked around the room. "Is that a storage closet over there?"

Gustaf opened his mouth to respond to Lund and, crouched in the closet, Claire gulped. But just then, the fire alarm went off and both of the men quickly left the room to see what was happening. Claire slipped out of the closet, softly closing the door behind her, and moved furtively to the room door.

Gustaf and Lund were checking the two grade seven classrooms located just beyond the pullout room. Claire waited until they ducked inside one of them to look around and then she quickly scurried down the hall in the opposite direction—the direction leading towards the front door, and tried to lose herself in the crowd of students and staff members who were already exiting because of the fire drill.

Meanwhile, Gustaf and Lund must have satisfied themselves that nobody had been left behind, because they'd turned around and were heading back in her direction! Claire decided that if she had to choose between being caught and being rude she'd choose to be rude and she elbowed her way fiercely ahead.

When Claire finally managed to reach the main door, she headed for her car, hoping that nobody had recognized her, and drove straight to Roscoe's house where Tia was working with Roscoe in Claire's absence.

Tia and Roscoe took one look at Claire's face when she came in and Roscoe headed for the kitchen. He returned in a couple of minutes with a cup of coffee for her. "Heah, Claih. You need dis. Two cweam, no sougah...wight?"

Claire smiled at him gratefully, but said nothing. She sipped her coffee for a minute, then pulled out her cell phone and, with trembling fingers, dialed the school number. Doreen answered.

"Doreen, what was the fire alarm about?"

"It was necessary," Doreen replied tersely.

"How did you know?"

"I heard...I have to go now," she said and hung up the phone, leaving Claire to wonder and to smile gratefully.

"What?" Tia asked. And she told them. Obviously, Lund would've had to check in with Doreen when he arrived to inspect the microwave, and Doreen had tried to warn Claire. That would've been the buzz she'd heard on her phone and ignored.

Chapter 26: Another Criminal Investigation

When Gustaf returned to his office with Lund who, in the excitement, had forgotten all about examining the closet where Claire had been hiding, Lund told him, "I have enough to write up my report now. I feel quite certain that this was no accident, Mr. Lennon, but I need to find out if the front border on that microwave shelf was still there when Lydia started working with the two children. Can you tell me which hospital she's in? I will call and ask if I can visit her."

"She's in the Royal Alexandra Hospital, and I don't know what their visitor policy is. According to Jessie's mother, she's in a lot of pain and her jaw is wired shut, but she can write." Gustaf thought for a minute and then added, "There's another possibility, though. Bertha, another classroom aide in the school, sometimes covers for Lydia and she might have used that microwave to warm her lunch instead of coming all the way down to the lunchroom to do it. You could ask her?"

"Good. Can you reach her now? I'd like to get this report wrapped up," said Lund.

Gustaf called Bertha on the intercom and she turned up in a few minutes. "I used that microwave last Tuesday," she said. "I don't think the shelf is completely level because the microwave often slides forward a bit, but there's a little board on the front of the shelf that holds it in place."

"There's no board there now," Gustaf said.

Bertha looked surprised. "It was definitely there on Tuesday. I remember because when I closed the door, the microwave slid and I remember thinking it was a good thing that the shelf had that rim."

"Would you be prepared to testify to that in court, if necessary?" Gustaf asked.

Bertha looked surprised and a little awed—but then she just shrugged her shoulders and said, "Sure. I *know* what I saw."

After Bertha left, Lund turned to Gustaf and said grimly, "my report will indicate that the microwave shelf should have been adjusted once the slant was noticed as that was a definite health and safety risk. The front border was a good idea, but it should only have been there as an additional safety guard, *not* the primary one." Lund went on to say, "I will also indicate that there are definite signs of criminal intent and that the police should be contacted immediately to conduct their own investigation. I will also note in my report that I informed you verbally of the need for their immediate involvement. It's not my job to contact them, but it *is* my job to let you know that I believe it's necessary."

Gustaf nodded his head mutely, thinking of all the further complications and disruptions and negative effects on the school image likely to result with even more police presence. Lund said his good-byes and left.

Chapter 27: A Setback for Angela

When the door closed behind Lund, the principal put his head in his hands, mulling over what to do. But he didn't have long to worry about it because almost immediately there was a sharp knock on the door. Gustaf opened it to find Angela Arietti standing there with a young woman beside her.

"We've been waiting a long time," she said abruptly. "I trust we can see you, now?"

Gustaf stepped back involuntarily and Angela swept in with the young woman in tow. "Gustaf, this is Monica Cummings. She works with Nico several evenings a week and is prepared to take over Lydia's position. Monica, this is Mr. Lennon, the school principal."

Gustaf looked stunned, but held out his hand automatically to Monica and greeted her. Then he turned to Angela and said, "As far as I know, Lydia is planning to return so we have no position open at present."

"Well, Monica can step in for the time being until she returns—*if* she returns. You're supposed to be providing an educational program for Nico, and I can't have him home any longer!"

Gustaf looked from Angela to Monica and searched desperately in his brain for an answer. "Actually, we've already arranged for a substitute."

Angela raised her eyebrows and looked straight at him. "Who?" she demanded.

"Bertha," he blurted out, hoping desperately that he could get to her before Angela did.

"She already has a full time job. Who's going to do that now?"

"Oh," Gustaf said smoothly, suddenly recovering the suavity that had gotten him this far in the first place. "There are substitute classroom aides available in the system able to take over on short notice with students presenting with the usual range of learning problems like the ones Bertha works with. And, fortunately, she covered for Pamela enough times that she knows Nico's and Jessie's programs." As an afterthought, he lied, "I've already been in touch with the board and have been assured that they'll have someone here Monday, so you'll only need to keep Nico home one more day."

Angela left shortly after in a huff and Gustaf, with trembling fingers, called the board office to see if anyone was available. He was not worried about Bertha. He had the power to just reassign her whether she liked it or not, but if he could not get a substitute in to take over her responsibilities right away, he'd be caught in his lie.

The secretary who answered the phone told him he'd need to send in an official requisition. Gustaf fumbled around his office searching through files to find the necessary form and finally had to ask Doreen for it. He didn't like to involve the school secretary in this matter, because the fewer people who knew that this request was going in only now, the less likely it was to get back to Angela. Doreen raised her eyebrows inquiringly when she handed the form to her boss, but Gustaf said nothing.

After laboriously filling out the form—and Gustaf had to call the school board secretary back for further directions—he fumbled with the fax machine as he tried to send it in, finally asking Doreen for help. She offered to fax it for him, but he declined, saying it was necessary for him to learn how to do it himself. Doreen raised her eyebrows again, but said nothing. In the three years she'd been working with Gustaf at this school, he'd always seemed quite happy to remain ignorant about anything clerical or technological—simply assuming that she could, and should, handle it.

Finally, the form, marked *very urgent* and *immediate response required* was sent and Gustaf waited anxiously for a reply. At 3:30, that afternoon, the call came. A substitute, Anne-Marie Cameron, would be at the school Monday morning at 8 a.m., and would report to the office for orientation. Gustaf hung up the phone quickly and called out over the school loud speaker for Bertha, hoping fervently that she'd not left for the day. Five minutes later, she was in his office and he informed her of the new arrangement.

Bertha was a seasoned school assistant in her early fifties and she did not take kindly to arrangements for her job responsibilities being made for her without prior consultation. She proceeded to present all sorts of reasons why the principal's plan would not work. But, in situations like this, Gustaf was in his element. He had the power and the *superior* knowledge, and he explained to her that she'd been hired as a qualified classroom aide and, as such, had the credentials to handle this situation.

"I've seen you a few times working with Nico and you're really good with him. Few people could do as well. I certainly can't risk hiring somebody unknown from outside to take over. You know how much trouble Pamela had."

"That's because she listened too much to his mother," Bertha snorted.

"Well," Gustaf responded politically, "be that as it may, *you* are the only one I can trust to do this job in Lydia's absence."

"Humph," Bertha grunted, but Gustaf could tell by her tone that his flattery had worked. "But my current job is not exactly *nothing*. I'll have to have at *least* a day to orient the new person."

"Fine," Gustaf responded, mentally calculating how he'd handle Angela during that time. "I can arrange for Jessie and Nico to return to school on Tuesday, then?"

"I suppose so," Bertha said, with just a mild note of peevishness in her voice to indicate that she was doing Gustaf a real favor.

Angela was clearly not happy when Gustaf called, but here again, he thought he had the upper hand. "School policy," he said. "Necessary time for orientation," he added. "Properly addressing student needs," he intoned.

Gustaf then called Claire and the parents of the two children who were presently under Bertha's care to explain what had happened and would be happening. There were questions, but nothing compared to what Angela had demanded of him and he finally hung up the phone after the last call, a happy and relieved man looking forward to his weekend.

Chapter 28: A Joint Investigation or Not?

At eleven o'clock Saturday morning, Claire knocked nervously on the door to Lydia's hospital room. Technically, visiting hours were not until the afternoon, but the desk clerk conceded that the doctors had already made their rounds and that no other medical interventions were scheduled for Lydia since it was the weekend.

Lydia was not alone, however. Her sister was there and she stared balefully at the intruder. Claire tentatively proffered the box of cream-filled chocolates she'd brought, her hand wavering between Lydia and Celia, as if asking permission. "I thought you might be able to manage these chocolates, Lydia. They're all soft."

Lydia smiled wanly and nodded her head in thanks, but didn't look particularly happy to see her. Celia continued to glower as if somehow her sister's injury had all been Claire's fault. "I thought you might like to know what's happening at school," Claire said.

There was no response, but Claire continued bravely. "Bertha is going to be taking over with Nico and Jessie for the time being, and the school board found somebody to take Bertha's place temporarily."

"They'd better make that permanent," Celia growled. "Lydia's not coming back!" Claire caught the irritated glance Lydia directed at Celia and said to herself, *Hmm, bossy older sister syndrome. I can work with that!*

Without missing a beat, Claire's face assumed an expression of shock and sorrow. "Oh, no!" she gasped. "Not again! Jessie is *so* fond of you, Lydia. She trusts you so much. And you've made so much progress with her!" Claire stopped herself for a moment and then said in a mournful, resigned tone, "It seems, every time she lets herself develop a deep relationship with someone, they disappear out of her life, just like the assistant she had in elementary school. If she loses you too, I don't think she'll be able to trust again. I'm afraid she's just going to give up and wait for all her problems to just take her away. A really bad seizure one day and that will be the end. She won't have any reason to go on!"

After another pause, Claire wiped a tear away, shrugged her shoulders and tilted her chin up. "It's just Dan and me. That's all she has in the end and I guess we'll just have to get used to it." Turning to Lydia, she said softly, "I hope you recover soon. This shouldn't have happened to a good person like you." And with that, Claire turned away and headed towards the door, but just as she reached it she heard a faint sound.

"Waih!" Lydia called hoarsely. Claire returned to Lydia's side. After glancing defiantly at her sister, Lydia grabbed her pen and notepad.

"If you find out who did this to me and who killed Pamela, I'll come back," she wrote.

Claire hugged Lydia tenderly. "I *know* you care about Jessie, but you have to do what's best for you. But I *am* going to find the killer!" She left the room then with one last glance from the door, noting the frustrated expression on Celia's face and the determined set of Lydia's broken jaw.

After leaving the hospital, Claire sat quietly in her car for a few minutes to compose herself. Everything she'd said to Lydia had been true, but it had been said for effect. She felt mildly guilty for playing on the emotions of someone in such a vulnerable state, but then she shook her shoulders to jar herself back to earth. It was very true that the only people Jessie could really count on in the end were her parents and they had to do whatever was necessary—within ethical and legal limits—to ensure that she had the best life she could have.

Claire reminded herself that she was not the only one putting pressure on Lydia. Clearly, her sister had been doing a pretty good job of that too. And before the accident, it had been quite clear that Lydia had been enjoying the new challenge of working in the school, and that it had been good for her in terms of preparing for her future planned career. This accident was just a bump in the road and shouldn't be allowed to derail Lydia's plans completely. Having talked herself into a relatively guilt-free state, Claire headed down the road towards Tia's house. They needed a strategy session.

Chapter 29: Reflecting on the Problem

Tia was surprised to see Claire but not unhappy. Fortunately, Tia's husband, Jimmy, an industrial electrician, had been called away on an emergency electrical breakdown at a brewery that was going to result in the destruction of their latest batch of beer if not resolved soon. Thus, he wasn't at home to glower at Claire as he usually did when she had the temerity to intrude on their weekend.

"We need to talk," Claire said, and soon the two women were sitting in the living room with cups of coffee. Claire told Tia what Lydia had said and then added, "If Lydia doesn't come back, this whole year is just going to be a wipe-out for Jessie! And the two of them were making such *progress*!" she wailed.

"Do you mean that Lydia was going to be able to get the best out of both Nico and Jessie?"

"No," Claire sighed. "It's still not right to have Nico and Jessie together. Their requirements are too different. Neither of them is really getting what they need."

"I thought you said that Lydia was doing well with them."

"She *is*—the best anyone could do under such ridiculous circumstances!" Claire added angrily. Tia just raised her eyebrows and Claire went on, "Nico can see. Jessie cannot. Nico is capable of learning much more than Jessie academically, but his behavior is so out of control that he's not learning. Jessie needs a lot of physical intervention and support every day to keep her muscles from just freezing up and to keep what skills she has—toileting, for example—intact. But there's no time for *that* because of the need to be constantly monitoring Nico's behavior."

"But maybe his behavior can be fixed! Lydia has already made some gains, you say."

"His behavior can never be fixed entirely because of his diagnosis."

"But, you don't know what kind of brain damage he really has. According to what Lydia saw of the specialist's report, Nico acts *like* individuals with Fetal Alcohol Spectrum Disorder. He didn't say that Nico actually *had* that diagnosis."

"He *couldn't* say it, Tia. It's a political hot potato! But, when we were in the Bahamas, Gus *heard* Angela's husband comment on her chronic drinking, including during her pregnancy. And anyway, Nico has many of the *physical* signs associated with FAS-D."

"Like what?"

"His eyes are close together; he has a short, flattened nose and a thin upper lip—and his ears are kind of low on his head and stuck out."

"So are Prince Charles' ears!" Tia interjected. "Does that make him a FAS-D victim, too?"

"No, there are all kinds of variations in how people develop physically. No one characteristic can lead to a diagnosis of FAS-D."

"Then why are you so sure that Nico has this diagnosis?"

"His behaviors are just like those of children I've met with FAS-D, or how I've heard the behaviors of children with this diagnosis described."

"And what *are* these behaviors?"

"I've heard parents and foster parents describe their children's problems with impulse control. For example, lashing out suddenly or taking huge risks with no thought of consequences. And they want what they want. If they see something they want, they just take it. It doesn't matter to them that it belongs to somebody else."

"Like Nico running away without any idea where he is going or what might happen to him as a result!"

"Yes, exactly."

"So, what's the answer for somebody like him? What kind of school setting should he be in where he'd be safer?"

"I don't know—but what I *do* know is that he's a lot more capable of learning academics than Jessie. He needs behavioral control and a level of academic stimulation appropriate to his capabilities. He also needs peers who are functioning at or above his cognitive level who could act as role models. And he definitely should not be paired with Jessie—for both their sakes."

"You said that Lydia was at least better able to control his behavior than Pamela was—or chose to be. What about Bertha? How do you think she'll do? She struck me as a tough, no-nonsense person."

"Yes. But that's not necessarily the answer."

"What? Are you going all touchy-feely now? I thought that was just what *didn't* work?"

"The three of them are on a continuum, with Lydia in the middle. Nico definitely needs to have his negative behaviors controlled, but he also needs to have his academic and emotional needs met, to find school interesting and challenging, and to feel that the people who work with him find him interesting and worthwhile as a human being."

"That's a tall order, but it sounds like if there's any hope of getting Jessie and Nico through this year in reasonable shape, we'd better find the killer so Lydia will come back to work."

"Exactly, but how do we go about doing that?"

"What about Pamela's husband? Do you know how to get in contact with him or could Doreen tell you? She must have a home address for Pamela. Maybe he's still there."

"Actually, it's right in the phonebook. I looked it up. It's not far from the school," Claire said thoughtfully. But just then her phone rang.

"Claire?" came a raspy voice through the phone line. "It's Karen. I'm sorry but I'm really not feeling well at all." A nasty coughing sound followed this pronouncement. "Could you possibly come back home and look after Jessie? I really need to leave."

"Oh-h," Claire groaned. "What about Dan? Isn't he there?"

"He is, but he says he has to go into the office for an urgent meeting with his new client."

"Okay," Claire sighed. "I'll be home in about 15 minutes."

Chapter 30: Flushing Out a Suspect

Claire drove home feeling angry and sorry for herself. Her life was always like this. At any moment, no matter what her plans, she could suddenly be held hostage to meeting Jessie's needs. She'd become used to measuring her day in chunks: the hours when she had an assistant for Jessie or Jessie was at school and the hours when she and Dan were responsible for Jessie. At any time, day or night, Jessie could need assistance. *How am I supposed to have a career or even a life of my own?* she asked herself.

Claire's emotions were intense but short-lived. She didn't adjust easily to new demands or changes of circumstances, and tended to react with sudden bouts of anger, despair and self-pity. But just as quickly, she could turn around and figure some way to make lemonade out of lemons. This occasion was no exception, and she suddenly pulled off to the shoulder, reached for her cell phone and called Karen back, directing her to get Jessie ready for a little trip.

Claire's reasoning went as follows. She needed to meet with Pamela's husband, Gil Burton, because he was the prime suspect or, at least, the only likely suspect in her death they'd uncovered to date. But what could meeting with him actually tell her? If she took Jessie, however, Claire would learn more. Although Jessie couldn't see or talk or communicate formally in any way, she seemed to have a sixth sense about people. Claire, who knew Jessie so well, could tell immediately by the look on Jessie's face and by her body language whether Jessie was comfortable or uncomfortable with a new person she'd just met. Moreover, she could sense whether Jessie was emanating discomfort and distaste only, or also fear and revulsion. And in this case, the fact that people invariably underestimated Jessie when they first met her would work to Claire's advantage.

Pamela's husband, Gil, wouldn't pick up on what Jessie was communicating and they'd be safe. Still, the only reason she was able to take Jessie with her on this venture, was because Dan wouldn't be home to stop her. It was a golden opportunity and Claire went from moaning over her lost afternoon of freedom to feeling very happy that things had worked out the way they had.

Pamela and Gil had rented an apartment on the fourth floor of a modest, six-story building. Fortunately, it had an elevator to accommodate the wheelchair and Claire sighed with relief when she saw it. Now, if only Gil was home. Claire had contemplated calling ahead, but decided it would give him too much opportunity to tell her he was busy. She rang the bell and waited.

The door opened and a tall, rather muscle-bound man with dark hair and a small mustache stood there. "Hello?" he said suspiciously, with raised eyebrows, glancing back and forth between Claire and Jessie. In a sudden flash of intuition, Claire could read what he was thinking. *We ignored the* no solicitors *sign at the door and are here ready to make a spiel for support of some obscure charity or other having to do with disabilities.*

"Hello," Claire answered. "Are you Gil, Pamela's partner?"

"I *was*, until she died," he replied.

"I'm so sorry," Claire responded. "I'm Claire Burke and this is my daughter, Jessie Marchyschyn. She was Pamela's student." Gil said nothing and Claire went on bravely. "We came to offer you our condolences and for another reason, too." Claire thrust the cake she was carrying towards him. This is a cinnamon-apple coffee cake I baked this morning for you. I hope you like it." Claire hoped that Dan wouldn't remember that she'd been preparing the cake before he left, originally planning on having it for their supper.

"Uh, thanks," he responded. "I suppose you better come in," he added, somewhat ungraciously. "I *am* expecting company shortly, however."

"We won't stay long," Claire assured him. Gil led them through to the living room and motioned at the chairs. Claire settled herself in an upright, rather low-backed armchair where there was room to place Jessie's wheelchair beside her.

"I'll just put this cake in the fridge," Gil commented. "Can I get you anything to drink?" Claire shook her head. "What about her?" he asked, turning to Jessie. Jessie oriented her face towards him with one of her delightful smiles. Gil smiled back involuntarily.

"Jessie's fine," Claire responded, noting the smile.

When Gil returned, Claire launched into her prepared spiel. She told him about Lydia and what had happened to her and how she was refusing to come back to work until they found Pamela's killer and the person who'd sabotaged the microwave causing the accident.

Gil listened carefully and then asked, "How do you know that the person who killed Pamela was the same person who sabotaged the microwave?"

Claire felt a chill come over her. *Was he saying this because he was the one who killed Pamela and he knew he hadn't touched the microwave?* That would make sense as his grudge was clearly with Pamela, according to what Claire had heard about the angry conversations he'd had with her at the school. Claire glanced at Jessie but she was still looking quite peaceful and comfortable.

Should she risk it? Claire asked herself, but then decided she had to. She calculated the distance to the door and surreptitiously unlocked Jessie's wheelchair brakes. "Several of the school personnel commented that you'd had a few altercations with Pamela at school and had been quite hostile towards her at times. Can I ask what these disagreements were about?" Gil looked very annoyed and Claire hastily added, "Any information you can give me could help me find the killer. I can't trust the police to do it. I don't think they have any leads to follow up."

Gil glared at her and replied, "That's really none of your business. In fact, this whole thing is none of your business. I don't know why you're even here!"

He started to get up, signaling that the interview was over, but Claire was not ready to give up so easily. "Why would you shout at Pamela in front of her students and fellow staff members for not ironing your shirt? That seems pretty mean to me!"

Gil's face changed from annoyance to incredulity to anger. "O-o-h! So you think *I* pushed her over that railing! Well, if I *did,* maybe I had..." The doorbell rang before he could finish his sentence and Gil moved to answer it, a look of disgust on his face. "That's the company I was expecting so...."

This was a clear message for Claire to leave, but she continued to sit there, needing to hear the end of Gil's last sentence. She had sneaked the occasional look at Jessie's face during the heated exchanges between them and saw no fear there—only mild tension when Claire raised her voice and curiosity when Gil replied. It seemed like Jessie was detecting honest outrage on his part, not hidden menace.

Gil opened the door and a young woman entered. She started to move into his arms, but he sidestepped away from her. Grudgingly, he turned to Claire. "This is a friend of mine, Elsie Tucker." Turning back to Elsie, he explained, "This here is Jessie," he said, wagging his thumb at her, "and her mother, Claire …uh…Burke?"

"A *friend*?" Elsie asked. "I thought we were more than that!"

Claire rose smoothly before Gil could reply, crossed the room and shook Elsie's hand. "Pleased to meet you, Elsie. I'm glad to see that Gil has found someone to take his mind off losing Pamela."

Elsie stared at Claire, speechless, and Gil glared daggers at her. Jessie picked up the negative vibes coming from him and began to fuss nervously. But Claire did not move, reasoning that Gil was unlikely to get violent in front of what was clearly his new girlfriend.

"You can think what you like," Gil snarled, "but maybe you'd do better by checking up on *Pamela's* boyfriend. He was on the scene a long time before Elsie was."

"I'd love to do that if *only* I knew his name," Claire said sweetly.

"I don't know it, but I'm pretty sure it was some guy right there at the school. Now, if you don't mind, I'd like to be alone with my *girl*friend." With that, Gil opened the door wide and then strode over, grabbed the handlebars on Jessie's wheelchair and wheeled her swiftly towards the door.

"But who? How?" Claire stuttered. Gil did not answer her. He gently pushed Jessie's chair out the door and then stood there, mute with his arms crossed, waiting for Claire to leave. She had no choice but to comply.

Chapter 31: Claire Digs for Answers

Claire drove by Tia's house on the way back home and longed to stop, but she could see Jimmy's truck in the driveway and knew she'd not be well received. Anyway, it was getting on towards supper time and she had to get Jessie, who'd been very patient, home. *Dan's back,* she noted to herself when they arrived at the house. Claire unloaded Jessie and took her into the house and directly to the washroom. Once Jessie was seated securely on her commode, Claire went in search of Dan. She just had to tell someone what she'd learned.

"You took Jessie to the home of a possible murderer?" Dan asked in a loud voice.

"I knew he didn't really do it," Claire said defensively, although she'd known nothing of the kind.

"That was totally irresponsible—and also very sneaky. You *knew* I would have stopped you if I'd been home!"

"Fine! But I learned something very interesting while I was there. Anyway, I need to go get Jessie off the commode and get her supper ready." Claire left, glad of the excuse.

Supper was a glum and silent affair with Dan fuming, Claire sulking, and Jessie, picking up on the mood, fussing away unhappily. After the dishes were done, Claire became very busy doing a second round of exercises with Jessie, even though she usually ignored that responsibility when she was alone with her. After Jessie was tucked into bed for the night, Claire watched an episode of *The Big Bang Theory* on the bedroom television, and then got ready for bed and turned all the lights out. Some time later, Dan came in. Claire was still awake but said nothing. She hated these rare disagreements she had with him, but had to stand her ground. There had been no other way she could see to move ahead with the investigation. She rolled over on her side and pretended to be asleep when she heard him come in the room. He crawled into bed beside her, turned away from her and said nothing.

Claire tried to sleep, but she couldn't. Finally, she rolled over, clasped her arms around his back and murmured, "I'm sorry but I had no choice. I knew Jessie would be able to tell better than me if he was the murderer. And I couldn't imagine him taking the chance of getting rid of both of us right there in his apartment. He'd have surely been caught. And besides," Claire added, "Jessie is part of this family and she should contribute, too, where she can. Everybody has to take risks in life sometimes."

Dan groaned. "To try to penetrate your logic is like walking through a forest blindfolded. You can always justify your actions—even when they make absolutely no sense to anybody else. But I know they honestly make sense to you. Just be careful, please."

"Can I tell you what happened?" Claire asked in a small voice.

"Su-ure," Dan said, resignedly.

Claire related the story, ending with Gil's suggestion that Pamela had had a secret boyfriend at the school.

"So how do you plan to find him? Because, I'm sure that's your next project! Are you going to go around and knock on every classroom door or make an announcement in the staff lunchroom?" Dan asked sarcastically.

"I don't know," Claire replied thoughtfully, "but I thought I'd get Aunt Gus and Amanda working on it for starters."

"You're crazy!" Dan said affectionately, as he rolled towards her. There were no more words between them that night and Claire thought afterwards that make-up sex really was the best!

Chapter 32: The Strategizing Gets Serious

The next day was Sunday. Claire and Dan worked together to get Jessie ready for the 10 o'clock service at their local United Church, and afterwards they went directly to Jimmy's and Tia's house where they'd been invited for Sunday lunch. Claire carefully carried in the breakfast hot-dish she'd made the night before and Tia placed it directly in the oven. Then they all sat down for coffee and a quick visit before lunch.

In a few minutes, Aunt Gus and Amanda arrived and Claire took the opportunity to tell everyone about the meeting she and Jessie had had with Pamela's husband, Gil, the day before. Gus and Amanda and Jimmy just shook their heads when they heard how the conversation had gone, but Tia was used to Claire's antics. The two of them had been through enough together that she knew you had to take risks and ask tough questions at times. The presence of Jessie at this meeting was upsetting to everybody though, and Jimmy gave Dan a quizzical look. Dan just looked back flatly. He had said what he'd had to say to Claire about that and he didn't feel like rehashing it in front of the rest of them.

At 11:45, Jimmy's sister, Mavis, arrived, pushed by her wannabe boyfriend, Bill. The two of them lived in the house across the street along with Roscoe, who'd gone home to his parents for the weekend. Jimmy took hold of Mavis' wheelchair and ushered her in, while John, the young staff member who'd accompanied them, handed Jimmy their offering to present to Tia, a batch of rather lumpy-looking brownies that Mavis and Bill had both helped to make. A horn honked in front at that moment and John quickly left to join his girlfriend in her car, glad to have the rest of the day off.

Soon the group was sitting down to lunch at the large dining room table with Aunt Gus insisting that Jessie sit next to her and bossily taking over the task of spoon-feeding her the pureed lunch Tia had prepared in advance for her and Mavis. Not to be outdone, Amanda asked if she could look after feeding Mavis and that freed Claire and Tia up to attend to serving the lunch for the rest of the group.

Claire brought out a huge 10 by 20-inch pan filled with her special breakfast dish recipe, a delicious combination of egg and milk-soaked bread, crisp bacon, three different cheeses, onion and red sweet pepper as well as judicious dashes of both cayenne and nutmeg. She set it down carefully on the four hot pads arranged to accommodate it and to prevent any possible damage to the beautiful tablecloth that Tia's mother had given her. Everyone oohed and aahed and Claire took a moment to just soak it up and feel successful for a change.

Claire had been feeling off balance since yesterday, wondering if she *should* have taken Jessie to Gil's apartment and if it *had* been necessary to confront him so bluntly. Her impulsive actions were often followed by attacks of conscience like this that left her feeling bad about herself. Claire now looked at her culinary creation sitting all puffed and golden in the center of the table and giving off a delicious aroma and thought to herself, *at least I can do* some *things right!*

There was silence at the table for a few minutes as people served themselves the quiche-like breakfast dish, Tia's delicious fruit salad livened up with the addition of mango and pineapple and a generous measure of Grand Marnier, Amanda's moist and tasty caraway rye bread and the tossed green salad that Aunt Gus had prepared. However, Gus soon broke the contented silence with a question. "So what did you actually accomplish with this rash act of yours yesterday, Claire?"

Claire gulped and said defensively, "Well, Aunt Gus, you know that Jessie has a sixth sense about people. You remember, Jimmy? She *knew* you were a good guy." Everyone at the table all looked towards Jessie who grinned and vocalized when she heard this. *Did she understand what I was saying?* Claire wondered, *or is she just responding to her name? I guess I'll never know,* Claire thought, sadly.

Claire went on speaking. "I think I learned two things we didn't know before. I'm almost certain that Gil is not our guy. I suspect that his nasty behavior towards Pamela at school came from his belief that she was having an affair. We also have a possible new lead. Gil seems to think that Pamela's paramour was somebody she met at school. Aunt Gus, Amanda, you're there every day and you see the various staff members. Have *you* any ideas?"

Amanda asked, "Why does this person have to be a staff member? There are consultants coming into the school all the time. I've seen at least three of them so far."

"That's true!" Gus piped up. "I was talking to a man in the staff room one day who said he was a speech and language pathologist." Gus hesitated for a minute and then said, "I don't know why he called himself that. I thought pathologists worked with dead people!"

"Professionals like their fancy titles!" Amanda added dryly.

"Probably, it's a way to align themselves with the medical profession and surround themselves with an aura of elitism," Jimmy added sourly.

"I wonder what the normalization crowd would think of *that* label." Claire mused. They're so obsessed with focusing on strengths rather than deficiencies—and you can't *get* much more deficient than by defining your entire discipline as a pathology!"

"I thought *you* were one of that crowd!' Tia said.

"No. I'll always fight for the rights of people with disabilities to live as normal a life as possible, but that does not mean pretending that they're normal!"

There was an awkward silence around the table and Claire looked from Jessie to Mavis to Bill.

Claire realized that she'd done it again, blurted out her thoughts without fully considering her audience first. And Bill, at least, was capable of understanding a surprising amount if you happened to catch him at a moment when he'd emerged from his autistic haze. However, she didn't pick up any negative reaction to her comment from the three of them and Bill was busy meticulously sorting and stacking the various vegetables in his quiche so he could eat each part separately.

Dan interjected at this point. "Pleasant as this is, we haven't got all day. We need to stop trashing this pathologist guy and get back on track. "Gus, I feel like you were going to say something more about him, about why he was there and who he was consulting with."

"It was one of the kids Bertha has been working with. I think his name is Larry. That consultant, Richard something or other, was talking about slow auditory processing speed. He was saying that this kid had so much trouble learning because he could only understand part of what anybody said. While he's trying to grasp the first part of what people are saying, they're still talking and he misses what they're saying next."

"Well, that definitely sounds like a lead worth following up on," Claire exclaimed. "But how? Could you and Amanda.... Wait, I have an idea!"

"Oh, oh!" Dan muttered.

"Its not what you *think*—and it *does* make sense," Claire retorted defensively. "Doreen was really helpful in keeping me from getting caught when I was checking out the microwave. She even called me when Gustaf and the occupational health and safety guy headed towards the pullout room, and when I didn't answer, she pulled the fire alarm to create a distraction. I think we could trust her to help us more openly at this point. Doreen might have heard things or be able to point us in the direction of somebody else who might know something." The rest of the group looked skeptical and Claire just said, "Well, it's worth a try, anyway."

Gus said self-importantly, "I will talk to her tomorrow when Amanda and I are there for lunch."

"No," Amanda said mildly. "*This* time, I think *I* will do it." An embarrassed silence followed from the group and finally, Claire said gently, "Aunt Gus, she must never, *ever* find out about the key switch!"

"*I* wouldn't say anything."

"I know you wouldn't do it on purpose, but it might accidentally slip out. Besides, you've had your adventure. Look at what you discovered in the Bahamas! Don't you think it's fair to let Amanda get in on the action, too?"

"I suppose so," Gus grumped. She turned to Amanda and said, "When we get back to the house I'll give you some pointers on how to approach Doreen."

"Uh, huh," Amanda said, and managed to keep her face in a neutral pose. But when Gus turned back to

Claire, Amanda could not keep herself from turning to Tia and rolling her eyes. Claire noted the exchange and saw Tia's lip twitch before she got control of it.

Chapter 33: Honesty: A New Approach To Getting Answers

That evening, Amanda listened patiently as Gus went on interminably about the best strategies for approaching Doreen. She nodded her head agreeably at the critical moments in the monologue and appeared to be taking in all of Gus's many suggestions thoughtfully. At school the next day at 12:30, she left Gus in charge of the senior high students and headed off to the office where, fortunately, she found Doreen eating her lunch at her desk so she could catch up on some work.

"Hi, Amanda! What can I do for you?"

"It depends. Got a few minutes to talk, assuming nobody comes in?"

Doreen raised her eyebrows. "It *is* my lunch hour and Gustaf has gone to a meeting at Central Office for the afternoon. I'll just close and lock the door. I *do* that sometimes during the lunch hour when I just don't feel like being disturbed." Doreen got up and locked the door. She motioned for Amanda to sit down in one of the comfortable waiting room chairs in the office. She took the other chair and continued eating her sandwich.

"Thanks!" Amanda said. "It's about Pamela—and about Lydia's accident last week."

"I thought as much. I've been waiting for you guys to open up to me."

Amanda was a bit jarred by this remark but not really surprised. She realized they'd not been exactly subtle, particularly Gus. "Lydia says she's not going to come back unless we find out who did these things,

Doreen. And I gather Lydia was really making progress with Nico, and Jessie was, of course, happy with her. They've worked together for quite a while, you know."

"I don't blame Lydia for not wanting to return," Doreen responded. "I'd feel the same in her position."

"Yes, I agree—but how are we supposed to find the person who's responsible for Pamela's death—and Lydia's accident—if they're related? Yesterday, Claire visited Pamela's husband. She took Jessie with her. She mentioned to him the incident Gus had told her about him coming to the school and bawling Pamela out for not pressing his shirt. He got really angry!"

"Wow!" Doreen exclaimed. *"That* took guts! And what about Jessie? Obviously, Claire wouldn't have asked him that if she didn't suspect him of being the murderer! Wasn't she worried? And why would she bring Jessie into a situation like that?"

"Claire is getting desperate. She said that she's run out of leads. And Jessie is really good at reading people, even if she can't see or talk."

"But *still!"*

"He didn't do it, Doreen! At least, that's what Claire says. Jessie didn't react to him at all, not even when he raised his voice when he got angry about Claire bringing up that incident. But something else did happen. His new *girlfriend,* Elsie something or other, came to the door, which obviously embarrassed him. He got all defensive and told Claire that if she wanted to find Pamela's killer, maybe she should look for Pamela's *boyfriend.* According to Gil, he was on the scene long before Gil even *met* Elsie, who was now his girlfriend."

"Wow!" was all Doreen could say.

"Uh, don't talk to anybody else about this. It wouldn't be fair to him," Amanda cautioned.

"C'mon," Doreen said. "If you want me to help you by collecting information, and I assume that's what you're getting at, then I need some bargaining chips. I can't ask people for information unless I have something to offer them back. Gil has absolutely no connection with the school now that Pamela's gone, so what can it hurt what people think of him?"

Amanda struggled with her conscience. She didn't believe in gossip, in talking about people to other people, but she also realized that that was what might be needed in this situation. School personnel were never going to talk to her about anything very significant—and they certainly weren't going to talk to a parent—Claire, for example. No, if they were going to get anywhere, they needed the help of an *insider* like Doreen. Claire had been right, as she often was.

Doreen read all this on Amanda's face as she watched the conflicting emotions pass across it. "Don't worry, Amanda," she said softly. "I'm not going to gossip for the sake of gossiping. And if I do have to share this *girlfriend* business, I'll do so discreetly and only out of necessity."

Amanda looked at her gratefully and started to speak, but just then someone banged on the door. "It's after one and I really have to open the door," Doreen said. "I'm going to start digging and I'll call you in the evening from home in a couple of days" Doreen said. "Trust me!"

Chapter 34: Doreen Comes Through

Two evenings later, true to her word, Doreen called. Amanda was quick to answer the phone, being alone in the kitchen, which was not difficult since Gus was engrossed in a nature program about feral cats. However, Doreen didn't want to talk and spoke only briefly. "I've found out a few things of possible interest. I've typed them all up with the contact person's information, and I'll leave it in a sealed envelope on the corner of my desk. Can you pick it up tomorrow at noon?"

"I'll be there just after 12:30," Amanda replied. "And thanks!" she added weakly.

The next afternoon, after their lunchroom duties were over, Gus and Amanda met with Claire and Tia at Roscoe's home. Claire sent Roscoe off to his room to work on a new reading exercise and assured him that later they'd all have coffee and cake together. Tia had brought over what was left of the cherry-cream coffee cake from Sunday's lunch.

Amanda gave Claire the notes Doreen had prepared and Claire made copies for everyone with the printer attached to her computer in a corner of the kitchen. Then the four of them sat in the living room to quietly read through them.

"You can certainly see why Doreen makes such a good secretary!" Tia commented. "These notes are very methodically laid out."

Claire didn't respond directly, but simply said, "Doreen has listed four different possibilities for a liaison with Pamela here. Let's consider them one by one."

"Number 1. Richard Dawson, speech and language pathologist. Three different people saw Pamela involved in intense conversations with him on three separate occasions. Norma Ellison, one of the grade eight teachers, stated she'd been on quite friendly terms with Pamela and had asked her what she found so fascinating about Richard. Pamela told her that her younger sister had an auditory processing deficit and she was trying to understand it better and to find out what the best form of remediation would be," Claire read.

"After a pause, Tia said, "That sounds pretty plausible to me."

"She could've made it up as a cover," Gus argued.

"It doesn't seem very likely, though," Claire countered. After a pause, she made a suggestion. "I think we should just rank order these four different contacts for now, and that will at least give us a starting point."

"Good idea!" Amanda said briskly.

Claire read the second entry: "Number 2. Bruce Ramsbottom, delivery man. He often drops off UPS packages at the school. Several individuals stated that he seemed drawn to Pamela, but Bertha reported that he'd also acted that way with one of the previous teachers as well. When I asked Nelly Ferguson, the teacher in Bertha's classroom, for more details, she said he was always trying to 'chat Pamela up' and acted like he wanted to 'get into her britches'. Nelly's an exchange teacher from Britain, by the way! Anyway, she said that Pamela was always polite to him but nothing more and once she heard her explicitly referring to her husband in front of him."

"Doesn't sound like there's anything there worth pursuing," Amanda commented.

The others agreed and Tia added, "He seems a less likely bet even than Richard."

"Moving right along," Claire said briskly, continuing to read from Doreen's notes. "Number 3. Gerald Kuhn: Reading Specialist. He consulted frequently at the school this fall because there were a lot of reading assessments to do. He seemed to have a particularly friendly relationship with Pamela that a number of people noticed, and I even noticed it myself. They kidded back and forth and even flirted a little. But it was so open that it's hard to believe there was anything deeper than that going on. At least, I doubt if that would be the way most cheating couples would act. I noticed him at her funeral. He looked sober and respectful and sad like the rest of us, but not exactly broken up."

"It could all have been an elaborate act," Gus speculated.

"I agree," Amanda added. "I've seen that game in some movies where a couple act like they're such good friends and have such an easy relationship with each other that they can pretend to flirt because nobody will take it seriously, but actually it's all a big smokescreen because they *are* really serious about each other."

"What about the funeral, though?" Tia asked. "If he was really deeply involved with Pamela, wouldn't there have been some sign of it in his response?"

"Well," Claire summarized, "if we're rank ordering them, I guess I'd say he was a more likely bet than the other two, but still not very likely to have been having an affair with her."

"I agree," said Tia stoutly. The others remained silent and Claire turned back to her paper. "Number 4. Brian Littner: grades eight to eleven drama teacher and grades ten and eleven English teacher. He's also the staff advisor for the school newspaper and the school yearbook. Pamela volunteered to work on the yearbook with him at the beginning of the year and, at first, they seemed to get along very well. Several teachers commented that she had lots of positive things to say about him in the staff room—about his energy and his enthusiasm and about how talented he was. But then she stopped working on the yearbook committee and she didn't mention him anymore. She didn't say anything bad about him. She just didn't say anything at all. And when they met, they seemed quite cool and formal with each other, whereas several teachers reported that they'd seemed very friendly earlier on. The school organized a memorial celebration for Pamela a couple of days after she died. All the staff and students were there and I saw him there, too. But he was way in the back and I couldn't see his face very clearly."

Claire read the few extra lines at the bottom of Doreen's message quickly. "Well, this is all I've been able to find out to date, but I'll keep asking. I hope it helps. Doreen"

Claire opened the remarks this time. "I think this guy may be a real possibility. His behavior and Pamela's behavior were quite peculiar. If you met someone and were strongly attracted to him, but couldn't afford to be noticed, it would be quite logical to withdraw and keep your relationship strictly outside the school. If you had strong feelings it would be very difficult to maintain the posture of a completely neutral relationship and it would be quite easy to go overboard in the other direction in order to hide your special interest."

"That makes sense," Amanda agreed. "I'd say he's our best bet of the lot." The others agreed.

"Well, what's our action plan, then?" Tia asked. "How do we find out more?"

Chapter 35: Claire's Action Plan

When Tia asked about an action plan, she noticed that Claire had a calculating look on her face, so Tia turned to her. "Okay, Claire. What are you thinking? I *know* that look."

"I was thinking that Jessie is spending too much time in her pullout room and not enough time in an inclusive classroom setting. Since she's blind, she has limited opportunities for observation and interaction in regular classes, but if she could be included in a drama class it might be a very stimulating situation for her."

"Here we go again!" Gus exclaimed. "You're getting really good at exploiting your daughter, Claire! Besides, what purpose would it serve? And who's going to go in there with her, anyway? Bertha can't be in two places at once!"

"Well, Aunt Gus, I thought maybe *you* could. I happen to know that the grade eight Drama class meets Tuesdays and Thursdays from 12:45 to 1:30, right after the junior high lunch break. They meet downstairs just two doors down from Jessie's and Nico's pullout room. Amanda, I'm sure you wouldn't mind covering the lunch room during those times so Aunt Gus could attend the class with Jessie, would you?"

"Oh, no. I'd be fine with that," Amanda replied, watching out of the corner of her eye to gauge Gus's response.

"But what would I *do* there?" Gus wailed. "I don't actually get along so well with the junior high students," she admitted. "What about a senior high drama group?" she asked hopefully.

"No, the principal would never go for that. And besides, you don't have to worry so much about the students. It'll be the teacher's responsibility to maintain classroom control and he's not going to allow them to be disrespectful to you if he's any kind of a teacher at all."

"Would I have to go to *every* class or could I skip some? Or maybe Amanda and I could take turns like we do with the lunch hours."

"You'd be like a volunteer classroom aide and, as such, you'd have the responsibility to be there all the time. Of course, if for some reason Jessie couldn't be present, then there would be no point in *you* being there, and I suppose if you were really sick she'd just have to stay out for that day. But the idea would be for you to sit there and get to know the man through his teaching, and maybe visit a bit during breaks and try to find out a little about him—*subtly!* But maybe you're right, Aunt Gus. Maybe it *would* be too much for you. Amanda, would you consider doing it?"

Tia hid a smirk because she knew exactly what Claire was doing. Aunt Gus bristled visibly when Claire said this. She informed Claire that she was much better equipped for this task than Amanda because *she* was the one with the interest in drama and also, of course, she was the one with the strong relationship with Jessie and would know what to do to keep Jessie calm and happy during the class.

"Great!" Claire said. "But remember, you have to be very careful not to get him suspicious. Don't even *mention* Pamela to him. You'll just be there to do a quiet character study and to observe Jessie's reactions to him. Then you need to report back to the rest of us. And remember the locker, Aunt Gus. Don't do anything rash. Remember that we may be dealing with a killer here."

Suddenly, Claire had second thoughts and worried that she was putting her aunt in a dangerous situation. Tia, who knew her so well, read the look on her face and jumped in. "Amanda, your job is going to be to remind Gus before every single class that she has to be careful. You know she might forget otherwise—like with the locker."

Amanda nodded and Gus sniffed. "I know what I'm doing," she said. But when she saw the three sober faces looking back at her, full of care and concern, she softened. "Okay," she said in a quiet voice. "I know I've been a bit foolhardy at times and I know that sitting in that class day after day, it might be easy to relax and get too familiar and let the cat out of the bag. But I promise you, I'm not going to do that. I'm just going to sit there and relax and focus on Jessie like that's the *only* reason I'm there. And I really *do* like drama so I plan to enjoy it. I'll save my thinking and speculating until after class. We'll talk about it together at home, Amanda, so I can sort out my thoughts and then I'll report the short version to you guys," she said, looking at Tia and Claire. Amanda nodded her head and the others smiled in a way that suggested they believed in Gus and believed she could do this.

Chapter 36: Claire Meets Brian

Once Claire had set her mind on something it was difficult to stop her. Gustaf tried to argue that it was too late to make classroom changes and that the class group had already melded and should not be disrupted. He pointed out that the drama teacher could veto the plan and then he'd be helpless to go ahead with it. He reminded Claire that Jessie's *peer group* was her grade seven class, and she could not be just parachuted into a grade eight class. He also observed that Gus was not a qualified classroom aide. But for every argument, Claire had a counter-argument and, finally, he conceded that if the drama teacher Brian Littner would agree to this *mid-term interruption,* he'd okay it. Claire agreed, but only on condition that *she* be allowed to talk to Brian about it first. Since Gustaf was basically on the lazy side and preferred to avoid hassles whenever possible, he didn't object.

Claire was secretly delighted at the chance to meet with Brian on a legitimate mission that had nothing to do with Pamela. She wanted to meet him in his professional capacity and not with questions about his personal life that would promptly put him on the defensive. She put on her *earnest mother's hat* and told him all about Jessie, how she was blind but really enjoyed hearing different people's voices, and how she couldn't talk or communicate directly, but seemed to understand a lot of what was going on around her. However, she didn't mention Jessie's *sixth sense*—how she seemed extra skilled at reading people.

Brian seemed to be very interested in what Claire was saying and early on in the conversation acted as if he was actually looking forward to having Jessie participate in his class. He seemed, like most people drawn to acting, to have a genuine interest in human nature and to enjoy meeting people with different problems and different approaches to life, all *grist for his mill*, no doubt.

Claire struggled with the question of what to tell him about Gus. She questioned the morality of talking about her aunt to a total stranger behind her back. On the other hand, Aunt Gus could be rather difficult at times and Claire didn't want Brian to become offended and end up kicking Gus and Jessie out of his class. Claire decided to go for the sympathy approach. She explained how Gus had longed to be an actor and how she'd made a special hobby out of analyzing the strengths and weaknesses of various actors on television dramatic series she enjoyed watching. Therefore, Claire suggested to Brian, she might get overly enthused and even offer her own opinion on various dramatic issues they were discussing in class and Brian might have to just remind her that she wasn't one of the students.

By the time she was through talking, Claire could see that Brian was intrigued by what she'd said about Gus, and that he was even looking forward to having *her* in his classroom. As she'd been talking, Claire had sensed that Brian might have been empathizing in some way with Gus and she studied him carefully. Brian was a slightly overweight, ordinary-looking man of medium height with dark brown, wavy hair, badly needing a trim. If he'd ever acted, himself, Claire speculated that it must have been in character roles. He was hardly leading man material. What she saw in his face was a slight air of uncertainty, insecurity even, which he covered up with spurts of garrulous conversation interjected into their discussion at intervals. In short, he was not a man Claire could ever have been attracted to and she doubted that Pamela would have been either.

At the conclusion of the meeting, Brian suggested that Jessie and Gus join the class the following Thursday. That would give him, he claimed, the opportunity to inform the other students on Tuesday that Jessie and her caregiver would be coming and to orient them a little bit as to what was involved. Claire gave him permission to share what she'd told him about Jessie, but asked that he not say anything about Gus as that really wouldn't be appropriate. Claire had already mentioned Gus's role in the lunchroom and how she'd had some difficulties managing the junior high students. Brian promised that he wouldn't share any personal details about Gus, and also that he'd take responsibility for talking to Gustaf and assuring him that this change would actually be a positive one. Having Jessie in the class would be a good experience for the other students as well as for Jessie.

Chapter 37: Prep School for Gus

Claire left Brian's classroom feeling very elated. She'd succeeded in her quest, and now she was able to relax and contemplate how this new arrangement could actually be a very good and enriching experience for Jessie. Nothing ever made Claire feel happier than when she was able to bring something positive into her daughter's very limited life. She just hoped that Aunt Gus could cope with the situation and not sour it for Jessie through her vanity or self-dramatizing remarks.

It was lunchtime at this point, and Claire headed to Roscoe's house where Tia was still covering for her while Dan was at home with Jessie. Her husband hadn't been happy about this, having already covered for her most of Thursday and Friday the week before, but Claire had stressed the importance of these meetings with Gustaf and Brian, focusing on what it could do to enrich Jessie's life, even though that hadn't been her primary purpose at the time.

When Claire arrived at the group home, Roscoe had just finished his lunch. She noted that he was looking rather unkempt and suggested that he might like to take a shower, his usual hygiene routine having broken down in her absence. Once he left to do so, Claire sat down at the table and suggested to Tia that they have coffee and some of the left over plum cake that the night staff person had made. Tia agreed but raised her eyebrows. They'd had several conversations around Claire's need to celebrate every little success with either food or drink, but Claire ignored Tia's censorious look.

For the next half hour, Claire regaled Tia with the morning's events, charged up as she was with dual feelings of smugness and happiness. In reality, Brian had not been difficult to convince and Claire suppressed the thought that he might have quite readily admitted Jessie and Gus to his class *without* her elaborate explanations. Claire needed to feel the full glory of this moment because more often than not she was judging rather than lauding herself due to some real or imagined misstep resulting from her impulsive nature.

Tia quite enjoyed hearing the story, however, and praised Claire for her tactics and her ingenuity in coming up with the plan in the first place. However, she did have a sober warning about Gus. "You better have a private talk with Amanda and ask her to help orient Gus before that first class. First impressions are very important and very difficult to undo when they go wrong. Amanda needs to rehearse with Gus how to best present herself every day between now and Thursday if any of it's going to stick."

"I agree," said Claire soberly. "I was on such a high I temporarily forgot about what a problem Aunt Gus can be, even though I shared some of her behavior traits with Brian. If she ends up being a character of derision for the students, it will contaminate the whole situation. But how can I get Amanda alone to talk to her?"

"I'm not even sure you're the best one to talk to her," Tia said thoughtfully. "You have your own social problems at times. I think *I* will have to do it. "Isn't tonight the night that Gus has back-to-back shows on TV that she just *has* to watch?"

"Yes, it's Monday. You're right!"

"Okay, I'll phone Amanda about five to eight and ask her to come over here. I'll say I need help and advice with some organizational and decorating issues. Those are areas of strength for Amanda, and Gus won't want to come along because she's not interested in household matters, and because she'll want to watch her programs."

"Okay, good luck," Claire said tentatively. "You're right about her lack of interest in household projects, but you know how nosy Aunt Gus is. She doesn't like to be left out of anything."

"Fine. If she comes over, I'll just say that I need Amanda to come with me to the hardware store and there won't be room for Gus because we'll have to fill up the back seat with the stuff we're going to buy."

"Okay, but you'd better be prepared to specify what it is and why you're buying it and then you'd better actually bring it home. Aunt Gus is always on the lookout for rejection and she's suspicious about people, almost expecting them to lie to her and exclude her."

"I guess it won't be as easy as I thought".

"Yes, but now that we've had this conversation, I can see that it would probably be even more difficult for me—so I guess all you can do is try."

Chapter 38: Aunt Gus Goes to School

When Gus heard that Tia wanted Amanda's help with some organizational and decorating issues, she was not in the least tempted to tag along. As soon as Amanda left, Gus popped a bowl of popcorn, took off her shoes, plopped her feet up on Amanda's sofa and prepared to enjoy her programs in splendid solitude on Amanda's big screen TV.

Meanwhile, Tia discussed with Amanda the possible pitfalls Gus might encounter in drama class and worked with her on some strategies she might use to get Gus ready.

"That all sounds good," Amanda responded, "but how do you propose that I get her to listen to me? You *know* how stubborn she is!"

"From what I've seen, she respects you, Amanda, and recognizes that you have certain skills she doesn't have. She's often entertained me with the way you brought the junior high students into line at lunchtime!"

"Has she?" Amanda asked in surprise. "She's never struck me as very good at giving credit to others."

"Well, she's a complicated person," Tia explained.

"I *know* that," Amanda replied softly. "I think I know her quite well at this point."

"Well, then, you know that when you approach her with the suggestions we came up with tonight, you'll have to be careful so that she doesn't feel she's losing face." Amanda nodded her head and when Tia looked in her eyes, she saw the wisdom and compassion there that she wished Gus had, for Claire's sake.

Tia's concerns about Aunt Gus's nosiness were never realized. Gus didn't even ask Amanda about what they'd done that evening. She was never really interested in other people's problems unless she sensed that there was some way that her involvement in them would cause her to be cast in a particularly positive light to others.

That was Monday evening. By Tuesday night, Gus had had enough time to think about it and was beginning to realize that she might need some pointers as to how to fit herself into the drama classroom. Characteristically, she wasn't even considering how Jessie might fit in or how she might feel about being cast into this strange, and undoubtedly boisterous, setting.

Amanda started by trying to simulate what a drama class might look like and what sorts of questions the teacher might ask of participants. Of course, this really was not an area of strength for her and, in a few minutes, Gus snorted in disgust and said it was time for *her* to play teacher and for Amanda to play student. This actually worked much better for it allowed Amanda to role model appropriate answers to questions without making it obvious that these were answers quite alien to Gus's sensibilities. When Gus asked, for example, if Shakespeare had written all the plays credited to him, Amanda raised her hand. "Yes, Amanda?"

"Jessie knows," Amanda said, and then proceeded to pass on what little she knew about the controversy surrounding Shakespeare's plays as if it had come from Jessie's mouth.

"That's ridiculous!" Gus sputtered. "*Everybody* knows that Jessie can't talk!"

"Yes, but who is the student: you or Jessie? Do you *really* want to act like you are back in grade eight again?"

Gus asked another question then: what nationality was Hamlet? But Amanda did not answer. "Why aren't you answering?" Gus asked in frustration. That's *not* a hard question. Don't you know the answer?"

"Yes, I know the answer, but it's somebody else's turn to answer." Gus looked at Amanda blankly. "Didn't they teach you turn-taking in kindergarten?"

"I never *went* to kindergarten," Gus replied.

And so it went—for a couple of hours on Tuesday evening and again on Wednesday evening and Thursday morning. Amanda tried her best to impart some basic social skills to a woman who'd wended her way through 70 plus years of living without them and to avoid causing offense in the process. It was an uphill battle and when Gus left the lunchroom with Jessie at 12:35 on Thursday, Amanda fervently wished her good luck, but was not at all sure the situation would work out.

Gus had one strategy that Amanda hadn't taken into account, however. When she felt threatened or off-balance, Gus had been hurt and rebuffed enough throughout her life to know it was best to lie low. Thus, for the first few classes, she was very quiet until one day, Mr. Littner asked a class question she well knew the answer to and suspected that few of the actual students in the class did. The grade eight drama class project for the fall term was to study Shakespeare's iconic play, *Romeo and Juliet* and then in the winter term to prepare the props and the play so that it could be presented in a shortened form at a one hour school assembly in April.

Brian Littner asked his grade eight drama class, "Why were the Montagues and the Capulets feuding in the first place?" After the predictable heavy silence from the rest of the class, Gus timidly put up her hand.

"Yes?" Mr. Littner queried. Fortunately, he didn't have the habit of addressing the students by name—which would have been rather awkward in this case.

"Jessie knows," Gus squeaked, remembering Amanda's suggestion. He nodded and Gus proceeded, recalling Amanda's advice to answer in short sentences with common words and to stop short of saying everything she actually knew on the subject. "Shakespeare does not tell you how the feud started. He just says that it's been going on for so long the original reason for it is lost. All the current generation knows is that they're supposed to hate each other, but they don't know why. Gus turned to Jessie and said, "Is there anything else, Jessie?" Jessie obligingly smiled and wafted her head from side to side that, with a little imagination, could be taken as a negative.

There was an odd snicker from the class, but Brian Littner scowled fiercely at them and the room quieted. He turned to Jessie and played along with what was clearly a pantomime. "That was a good answer, Jessie." Then he addressed the class in general. "Does anyone think that kind of enduring feud between families could still happen today?" This precipitated a lively discussion with somebody mentioning the Sicilian vendettas and speculating that maybe the Romeo and Juliet story was one example of this. Gus wanted to mention that Verona, the setting for Romeo and Juliet, was in the north of Italy, but she remembered Amanda's warning not to say too much. And Mr. Littner, himself, then made this clarification.

After the class broke up, several students came up to Jessie to tell her she'd made a good point and they smiled at Gus in the process. Gus, in turn, felt that she was learning a lot about effective social interactions and only wished she'd had learned those lessons a while ago, like maybe 65 years earlier.

Chapter 39: The Consultant Who Only Consulted

The next two weeks passed without much happening
and the fall term was well advanced. For the most part,
Jessie seemed content in the classroom, but once in a
while, Gus had to take her out when she became too
fussy and disruptive. On one occasion, she had to find
Bertha because Jessie clearly wanted to go the
bathroom and Gus didn't think she could handle it, but
otherwise the integration seemed to be going pretty
well, and Gus was beginning to understand why Claire
had always been so keen on it.

Meanwhile, Claire, Amanda and Tia were following
up on other leads they'd received when they could.
Thanks to an advance warning from Doreen, Claire
arranged to be at the school on the day that Gerald
Kuhn, the reading specialist, was scheduled to be there.
Claire and Doreen popped into the staff room while he
was sitting alone, eating his lunch, and Doreen
introduced him to Claire. With calculated timidity,
Claire asked if she could talk to him a few minutes
about her *niece*, Leslie, who was only five, but seemed
to be already showing signs of a learning disability of
some sort. Gerald graciously told her he still had a few
minutes before his next scheduled classroom
observation. In fact, if he came into class late, it
wouldn't really matter. That often happened, he
claimed, because he usually needed to visit several
classrooms in the course of a day and he always entered
quietly, sat down at the back of the class and observed.

Claire launched into her prepared speech, doing her best to make it sound spontaneous. "It's like this," she blurted out, "Leslie's quite quick to learn in many ways. She knows all her numbers, for example, and can easily count to a hundred. But when she tries to write, she often works from the right to the left side of the page, and I've noticed that she reverses the numbers *2* and *3*, and the letters *b* and *d*."

"It does sound like possible dyslexia," Gerald conceded, "although without actually working with her I couldn't say for sure. Young children frequently learn skills at uneven rates."

"What I'm wondering," said Claire, "is what to tell my sister. Gertie doesn't see any problem, but I don't think she *wants* to see the problem. And I *know* early intervention is important."

"I wouldn't worry if I were you," Gerald soothed. "Something that classic is bound to be picked up very quickly at school and there are lots of learning resources available to help children overcome that problem these days."

Claire looked at him. "Do you just work with children with mild learning problems like this, or do you also work with more severe cases?"

"Well, I'm a reading specialist, so I either work with people who can read but have difficulties, or with people who potentially *could* learn to read if they had the right sort of assistance. Why do you ask?"

"I was thinking about the little boy who shares an assistant with my daughter, Jessie....Nico."

"Ah, yes. *I* remember Nico! His assistant, Pamela, asked me to assess him, and I saw him briefly in late September when I was here assessing another student. Pamela felt that he was capable of more intellectually than he was displaying."

"Oh, that's what *I* think, too! But then Pamela died, and I guess nobody's following up with you now about Nico," Claire said. "That was so horrible!" she added.

"Yes, I still can't believe it. Pamela was so full of life. We kidded back and forth all the time," Gerald said sadly.

"Oh? Had you met her *before* you assessed Nico, then?"

"No. Just this year—just a few weeks before she was killed, actually. But I really liked her. As a matter of fact, if she hadn't told me that she was in a committed relationship, I probably would have asked her out."

"When was the last time you saw her before she died?" Claire asked, a bit too eagerly.

Gerald looked at Claire suspiciously, but finally answered. "I think it was just a couple of days before it happened, on the Tuesday. But I was so busy I didn't have enough time that day to say more than a quick hello in passing. I wish now I had," he said sadly.

"I was there when it happened," Claire said soberly. I heard her *fall."*

"I heard she was pushed. Did you *see* anything? I'd sure like to see whatever monster did this get what he deserves!"

"Unfortunately, I didn't see anything. I was down the hall with Jessie outside her classroom door."

"Ugh," he said. "That 's too bad!" He sounded genuinely disappointed. Claire decided he was not a very good suspect.

Chapter 40: Delegation Saves Frustration

Amanda's assigned task was to find out more about the deliveryman who'd seemed to have a strong attraction to Pamela. Unlike the other three members of their little group, Amanda felt not the faintest need to prove anything. She believed in delegation, collaboration and energy-saving in general. She also believed in thinking before acting and not playing the hero—except perhaps for that one time when she'd grabbed a frying pan to fight off a man who'd attacked Gus. But, even then, she'd chosen carefully—a heavy cast iron pan that required two hands to wield it effectively, instead of a hammer or baseball bat that could have easily been snatched out of her grasp and then turned against her.

After some contemplation, Amanda decided that the best way to approach the deliveryman was not to approach him at all. Instead, she decided to get somebody else to do it, somebody who'd already met him a few times and therefore could at least recognize him when he came around. That somebody was Doreen. Thus, instead of planning some elaborate strategy, Amanda baked cookies. She decided to take some of these as an offering when she casually dropped in on Doreen at lunchtime the next day, and store the rest in the freezer for surprise visitors. Amanda believed in killing two birds with one stone as a part of her energy conservation policy.

As she collected the ingredients for the cookie dough, Amanda mulled over the strange collection of people she'd come to know since the death of Jimmy's first wife, Megan. Out of all of them, Gus was the greatest enigma: arrogant and selfish in some ways, but fragile and generous in others. And then there was her niece, Claire. Claire came across as earnest and dedicated—to her daughter's cause and thus, the cause of many others. Claire projected an aura of restless energy and chronic impatience, but spent little of that energy on herself. She was slightly overweight and dumpy looking at this point as a result. It was, Amanda concluded, as if Claire didn't feel that she was worth looking after.

Tia was a nice enough person who seemed to know who she was and where she was going—unlike Claire who came across as still searching and unfinished. But Tia *could* be a little on the smug side when it came to cleaning, or baking her endless cakes—all faithfully recreated from the recipes in the *Company's Coming Cake Book*. *The cakes were fine*, Amanda thought, as she mixed the cookie dough. But Amanda was a slender person who didn't believe in eating the cakes she made—*too little nutritional value, too many calories, and too easy to have that second piece,* she thought. With cookies, you could add extra healthy ingredients and reduce the unhealthy ones, and they kept much longer than cake. You could freeze them, and then pull them out for company, and even refreeze the leftovers so you didn't risk eating them.

But for the cookies she was making for Doreen, Amanda decided to just follow the recipe in her book. There was no need in this case to worry about making them particularly healthy and nutritious. That would just take more mental energy on her part and result in her talking to Doreen about the ingredients in the cookies, instead of about how to approach Bruce, the deliveryman. Amanda pulled out her *Company's*

Coming Cookies' book, that she'd surreptitiously purchased after people had made such a fuss over Tia's cakes, and got to work.

The next day, Amanda visited Doreen shortly after 12:30 when the senior high lunch hour started and Gus took over her post, freeing Amanda. Amanda had mulled over the best approach to take, but decided it was simplest to just be honest. Doreen thanked her for the Pecan Crunch cookies, and after tasting them, commented on how good they were.

"I'll photocopy the recipe for you, Doreen, if you like." Doreen nodded, her mouth still full of cookie. Amanda went on, "But now, I'd like to ask you about the delivery man who seemed interested in Pamela. We divided up the leads you gave us and questioning him was supposed to be my project. However, I honestly don't know where to start."

"Oh, he's quite friendly and approachable," Doreen replied. "As a matter of fact, he likes to talk a little too much."

"Yes, all that's fine," said Amanda. "But I've never met him, and I never met Pamela so how can I possibly bring her into a casual conversation with him? And besides, I'm only here at lunchtime and he doesn't exactly follow a schedule for delivering parcels."

"That's true," Doreen said, thoughtfully.

"You know, Doreen. It would make much more sense if *you* did it. *You're* the one most likely to see him when he drops off a parcel. He does bring them to the office, doesn't he?"

"Yes. They have to be signed for, so there's proof of delivery."

"Well, you said he likes to talk. Could *you* talk to him about Pamela? After all, you *both* knew her."

"I could," Doreen said slowly, but Gustaf might overhear me, and I don't think he'd be happy to know that any of us are snooping around trying to solve Pamela's murder case."

"What about telling Bruce that it's time for you to take a break and asking if he'd like a cup of coffee with you in the staff room? If it's during class time, there likely won't be any teachers in there then."

"Well, sometimes a teacher or two will be there if they have a spare period–but I guess it wouldn't matter too much if they heard us talking casually about Pamela. And Gustaf doesn't usually come into the staff room. He seems to be of the opinion that administrators and staff members should not mix casually."

"Humph!" Amanda said disdainfully. But after a pause, she added, "Will you do it? We think he's our best lead at this point."

Doreen looked intrigued, but she hesitated. "I wouldn't know what to say to him without making it obvious what I was doing."

"I can help you," Amanda offered. "I can prepare a list of questions you'll need to ask him and write down some possible ways of approaching him. We can even get together outside of the school and rehearse it if you like. I live close to the school and you could come over to my place after work today or tomorrow so we could prepare."

Just then, somebody knocked at the office door and Doreen said, "I have to get that. Lunch hour's over. Let me think about it and I'll call you tonight. Just write down your number for me, please," and Doreen handed Amanda a pad and pencil as she rose to open the door.

Amanda had to be content with that and she returned to the lunchroom, feeling reasonably confident that her mission had succeeded.

Chapter 41: Claire Thinks of a New Angle

Claire was taking the opportunity to catch up on some paper work since Roscoe had gone away on DATS for his afternoon at the East Wind Rising Art Centre which he'd attended twice a week for the past year. Most of the people who attended were required to have assistants with them, but Roscoe was so polite and self-directed that Sarah Hughes, the Director, had made an exception in his case after his first year of attendance.

Claire's mind wandered from her paper work, the most boring and tedious part of her job by far, and a memory suddenly popped into her head. One of the Senior High girls had commented to Amanda that she'd seen Pamela at a popular Vietnamese restaurant nearby, having lunch one day. Pamela had told the girl that she was really interested in trying out different ethnic foods. And somehow, in the heat of everything that had happened recently, Claire had dropped this tidbit of information completely out of her mind! She picked up the phone excitedly to call Tia.

When Tia answered, Claire blurted out, "We've been overlooking something. We were led astray!"

"I'm fine, Claire. Thanks for asking—and how are you?" Tia responded sarcastically.

"Listen!" Claire hissed. "Pamela's husband said she must have met her lover at school—if she even *had* a lover. But how could he *know* that? And *we* just took it as fact!"

"*You* may have done so, Claire, but *I* never gave it another thought!" After a pause, Tia added, "What are you getting at?"

"Pamela liked ethnic food. And people find favourite restaurants where they feel comfortable and know they can count on food they enjoy. What if Pamela went off to a nearby restaurant on some of her lunch breaks? What if she *met* somebody there?"

"It's not impossible," Tia acknowledged. "But even if true, how would you ever identify him?"

"Internet! I'll check all the ethnic restaurants near the school. I'll get a picture of Pamela and go there and ask if they recognize her!"

Tia shook her head skeptically. "Sounds like a long shot. And anyway, I don't think assistants get very long lunch hours."

"Well, I don't have any other leads that look remotely promising, so I *have* to do it!"

"Okay, do you want me to help?" Tia asked with a distinct lack of enthusiasm.

"Claire hesitated before speaking. "You don't seem nearly as eager to work on this murder investigation as the ones we've dealt with in the past, Tia."

"I have other things on my mind right now."

"Are things okay between you and Jimmy?" Claire asked tentatively, recalling the big fight Tia and Jimmy had had over their Mérida escapade last spring when Tia and Claire had been trying to help Roscoe.

"We're fine," Tia said. Claire was about to inquire further when Tia blurted out, "I think I am pregnant!"

"Wow!" was all Claire could think to say. "Have you seen the doctor yet?"

"Tomorrow," Tia responded tersely.

"Does Jimmy know?"

Claire heard a voice in the background and then heard Tia sing out, "Okay, Jimmy. I'm coming!" Into the phone she whispered, "No. I'll call you tomorrow night. I have to go."

Tia hung up and Claire sat there stunned. If this were really happening, everything would be different now. Tia would be busy with the baby and there'd be no more time for cosy chats and no more appetite for participating in their wild adventures together. Claire realized with a start that she was feeling jealous— jealous of a baby who might not even exist. She suddenly knew how much Tia's friendship had filled a huge gap in her life and how much she'd come to secretly regard Tia as the sister, the family, she never really had.

Pathetic! Claire scolded herself. She should be happy for them and for Jimmy especially. Claire knew he'd come to love Tia's son, Mario, but still he must want a child of his own, a child with Tia, after all the sadness from his first, unhappy marriage. *I'll move on,* she told herself.

Chapter 42: Bill and Roscoe Go to Work

Monday morning came all too soon and Claire prepared Jessie for school with a heavy heart. Jessie was certainly happier with Bertha than she'd been with Pamela, but it still wasn't good—not like it had been with Lydia or like it had been in Jessie's old school with her previous assistant. Bertha did a competent enough job in terms of carrying out the exercises and taking Jessie to the bathroom regularly. But she was very clearly just doing her duty and not enjoying it very much—and Jessie felt this keenly. So she still came home acting sad and dull, even if her limbs were not as stiff as they'd been under Pamela's minimal care. And it took Claire, or Karen if she was there, most of the evening to jolly her into a better mood.

Well, Claire said to herself, *nothing negative is happening at school at least. Maybe I'll visit Lydia and try once more to convince her to come back. She's been home for a couple of weeks now and she must be feeling at least somewhat better.* Just then, Jessie's bus came and, after seeing her off, Claire quickly prepared herself for the day.

Today was actually a special day because Bill would be starting his internship as a cook's assistant at the restaurant. It had been open for two months now and was running quite smoothly so it was now possible to do some of the on-the-job training Claire had been thinking about for months.

Roscoe would be coming, too. He'd begin working with Mandy, the day cashier, to see if his many months of extra arithmetic training had helped enough to turn him into an effective money changer. The morning staff, who usually left for the day after Bill and Mavis were on the DATS buses headed to their day programs, would still be at the house getting Bill and Roscoe ready for their big adventure.

For a long time, Claire had been wanting to take over the day program component for Bill, but with so many different issues to work out when the group home first started operating and with the restaurant just getting established, it hadn't been feasible up to now. But today was the day she was going to try out her little idea. She got to the house at 9:15 and shortly after that, the three of them left for the restaurant in Claire's van.

When they arrived, Roscoe went directly to take up his place with Mandy. Claire had acquired a basic calculator with large numbers on it for him to practice on at home and he had that with him. It was a plug-in model but was also able to run on batteries, and new batteries had been installed for the occasion.

Mandy greeted him warmly; after all, Roscoe *was* her boss as he owned the restaurant! A small desk and chair had been set up behind the cash register and Roscoe settled himself there with his calculator ready to *shadow* Mandy, as Claire had explained he would do. He was just to watch what Mandy did for the first part of the morning and then, for the second part when customers slowed down, he was to try doing a shadow version of the transactions while Mandy did the real version. After each transaction, Mandy would check his work and advise him on any errors. With her watching, he was then to practice the same transaction over and over until such time as another customer was waiting to be served.

Claire had already gone through all this with Mandy in private, but now she reviewed it again while Bill and

Roscoe waited patiently. They watched as Mandy prepared a receipt for a client purchasing two coffees, a piece of coconut pie and a cinnamon roll. Roscoe just shook his head when he saw how fast Mandy added up the items on the cash register. "I not fast like Mandy, Claih," he said mournfully. People not be happy with me, not patient like *you*!"

"Roscoe, you will get much faster with practice. *I* was really slow at first, too," Mandy said.

"And you can sit there and practice as long as you need to," Claire said soothingly. "Mandy doesn't start her school program until January, and by that time I'm sure you'll be ready to take over for her. And *I'll* be here to help for as long as you feel you need me. Also, you're only going to be doing this three mornings a week, and the other mornings we'll practice whatever your weak spots are."

Roscoe still looked doubtful and Claire added, "I *know* you can do this, Roscoe! You have a head for numbers. I've *seen* it!"

Roscoe smiled at that, pleased with the compliment. Claire caught Mandy's eye and Mandy gave her a slight nod. She turned to Roscoe and said, "Okay, Roscoe. It's time for us to get to work. Bill and Claire better go off and do their thing and stop distracting us now," and she nodded dismissively at Claire. Roscoe grinned at this and settled back happily in his chair. Claire took the hint and she and Bill left for the kitchen.

Chapter 43: Building a Career for Bill

Bill was not especially interested in food. Roscoe was the one who was more passionate about it. But Roscoe didn't have the fine motor control to handle knives efficiently, and Bill did. Also, Bill enjoyed detail work that Roscoe didn't. So, according to Claire's calculations, this arrangement should work. Her schemes often did—but not always—and she watched nervously as Bill and Daisuke greeted each other in the kitchen. Roscoe's uncle still had an accent, but Claire was hoping that Bill would be able to understand him if he kept to simple, repetitive instructions. Claire had already met with Daisuke a couple of times to do some advance coaching and he certainly seemed eager to embrace the challenge.

"You help me. I need your help. I teach you how, Bill!" Daisuke said.

Bill looked at him and after a pause he nodded. *A good start,* Claire thought, *given his limited communication skills.*

Claire then introduced Bill to Scott, the regular assistant for both Daisuke and Satou Botan, who usually came in only in the afternoons to prepare for the evening meals. Botan's Japanese accent was much heavier than Daisuke's, so Claire didn't think it would be possible to develop a relationship between Botan and Bill.

"Hi," Scott greeted Bill casually, flipping his hand in the air in an abbreviated wave. Then he turned to Daisuke and said, "Look, I can get him going on something so you can focus on the cooking, Daisuke. "I'll start him peeling those carrots," he said, gesturing at the huge pile of carrots that needed to be prepared for the carrot soup on the lunch special. "That should be simple enough for him."

Claire narrowed her eyes when she heard this and if Dan or Tia had been there they would have recognized what she was thinking. She turned to Bill, who'd been completely left out of this conversation. She'd already noticed the troubled look on his face. "Would you like to work with Daisuke or Scott, Bill?"

After a pause, Bill responded in words this time, "Daisook. I work with Daisook. I *know* Daisook."

If Roscoe had been asked the same question, he would've had sufficient social sensitivity to soften his response somewhat, but Bill didn't have that particular facility. Claire also thought to herself that Bill didn't have the temperament for it either!

Claire turned to Scott and said softly, "I guess Bill will feel more comfortable right now working with Daisuke, Scott, but thanks very much for offering to help him. Maybe later on, he'll feel like working a little with you as well." After a breath, she added, "By the way, I think the carrots *would* be a really good place for Bill to start. Don't you agree, Bill?" Claire asked, turning to him.

Meanwhile, Daisuke was very carefully stirring zabaglione custard in a large double boiler on the stove. "Could Scott take over there for you, Daisuke, while you help Bill?"

Daisuke looked concerned. "This is a really delicate operation. It can go wrong in a second," Daisuke replied. "Maybe it would be better if *you* started Bill out on the carrots, Claire, and I can take over once this is finished. I don't have too much else to get ready today except to start the base for the carrot soup."

Daisuke turned to Bill and said, "Would that be okay with you, Bill?"

Bill nodded, a relieved look on his face. Claire suspected that this whole interaction had been a bit too complicated for him and that was why he was looking overwhelmed. She was anxious to stop all the words and get him involved in a simple task so he could feel comfortable and like he had a real place in this kitchen.

Claire asked Daisuke where they could work and he designated a generous counter space, knowing that Bill would want more space than usual. Claire guided Bill to the work sink and stressed the importance of washing their hands well and then putting on food gloves and clean aprons. She'd already asked him to wear a short-sleeved shirt that day. "Now, Bill," she said. "It's important that you not touch anything from here on in but the food and the sink. Don't touch your nose or even your face and don't scratch anywhere! We have to be very, very clean or the food inspector could come and shut us down. And worse still, we could make people sick who aren't used to our germs. Everybody has different germs, you know!"

Scott, overhearing this, scratched his nose and sniffed. Unfortunately for him, Daisuke saw this little scenario, turned to Scott and said sternly, "The same rules apply to you, Scott. Everything Claire says is true. We could easily lose our license if we aren't dealing with food according to government hygiene standards. I already had to let one person back here go because of that—and he was very good, too!"

Claire got very busy shaking carrots out of the bag and sorting them into piles of ten and worked hard to keep a neutral expression on her face. But she was very pleased at what Daisuke had said because it reinforced the message for Bill and made it clear that the rules did not just apply to him because he was *different*, something he was quite aware of. She was also very happy to see Scott put in his place because she could already sense the way his mind was working with reference to Bill.

"How many carrots do you want to work with at one time, Bill?"

"Ten," he replied.

"Okay," she said and she showed him the five piles of carrots she'd already arranged in piles of ten since she knew what his answer would be in advance—10 being his favourite number. "Now, I think the easiest way to do this is to take the skin off the carrots first and trim them and then wash them. What do you think, Bill?"

"Okay, but where the skin go?"

Claire was prepared for this and pulled out the newspaper she'd brought along just for this purpose. She separated a couple of sheets but then frowned, looking at the diminished counter space. But Daisuke had seen what was happening and he grabbed the newspaper and set it down at one end of a large worktable. Then he placed one pile of carrots and the vegetable parer and knife beside it.

Bill frowned. "Was that the first pile, Claire?"

"Yes, Bill. Daisuke did it right!" and she turned and smiled at Daisuke, thinking to herself how clever she'd been to work with him in advance.

Claire moved to the table and motioned for Bill to stand beside her. "Okay. This is what I do but maybe Daisuke does it differently. Let's try my way."

Claire grasped a carrot, wedged it against the table and ran the parer smoothly down it from top to bottom as far as she could get. Then she turned it upside down and pared from the bottom to the top. After this, she put it flat against the work table which was basically a large chopping block, grabbed the knife and using both hands carefully chopped off the top and the bottom using her palms to guide the flat back of the knife. This wasn't the way she would've done it at home, but she wanted to make sure that Bill would be absolutely safe from cutting himself and she saw Daisuke glance over and smile approvingly. Out of the corner of her eye, she also saw Scott with a slight sneer on his face. Daisuke missed that as Scott probably intended.

Chapter 44: A Pair of Parers

Bill propped the first carrot against the table and ran the parer down the side. It chipped off the edge of his fingernail and he looked upset. Claire patiently readjusted his fingers and he tried again. After five separate readjustments on Claire's part, he had more or less removed the peel from most of the middle of the carrot.

Claire looked in despair at the pile of carrots they needed to get through. She caught Daisuke glancing from them to the ragged-looking carrot Bill was holding with a worried look on his face. Claire grabbed another carrot and turned to Bill. "Okay, Bill. This time I'll help you."

"But we not finish. Have to finish carrot," he replied, looking agitated. Scott snickered but thankfully Bill didn't hear him because he was focusing anxiously on the half-peeled carrot.

Claire gave her head a shake to clear her focus. She was there to orient Bill, but the carrots had to get peeled even if she had to do the last 49 herself. How could she do this without getting Bill so anxious that he had a melt down? Why had she ever thought that she could just turn him over to Daisuke? She turned to Bill.

"Okay, Bill. This is what we're going to do. There are five different stages to peeling carrots and preparing them for the delicious soup that Daisuke is going to make. You're going to do stage one, peel the middle. I'm going to do stages two and three, peel the ends and chop off the top and bottom and drop them in the sink.

Scott will do stage four, rinse them and stack them back up in piles of ten, and Daisuke will do stage five, chop them up in pieces." She looked at Daisuke as she said this, and he nodded and then glanced meaningfully at Scott.

"But I have to finish. Have to finish carrot," Bill retorted, his voice rising again in agitation.

Claire said nothing but quickly grabbed the carrot, peeled the remainder including some missing middle shreds, chopped off the ends quickly while holding it and dropped it into the sink full of clean water. Daisuke saw what was happening, pointed to a clean spot on the counter and looked meaningfully at Scott. Sulkily, Scott grabbed the carrot from the water, lifted it out and languidly transported it across to the designated counter area.

"Water! Water drip!" Bill shouted—and Claire could see that his agitation was growing. Scott turned away but not before Claire saw the smirk on his face.

"Wipe it up!" Daisuke growled at Scott. "And next time do it right: shake it first and move quickly."

Claire grabbed another carrot, took hold of Bill's hand and focused him on the task. "This time, I help you", she said. "We do it together." Slowly and smoothly, she guided his hand up and down the carrot with the parer until they were in a soothing rhythm. Then she quickly finished it on her own and dropped it in the water. Scott snatched it, shook it and flipped it onto the counter. Bill looked concerned, but Claire focused him on the third carrot, proceeding hand over hand with the paring. Without looking up, she said, "Scott, you can just wait until we've peeled a bunch and then stack them in piles of ten, please."

There was no more talking after that. Claire knew that the best way to get Bill back into a relaxed state was to maintain silence and just proceed rhythmically with the task at hand. Once an additional eight carrots were in the sink, she suggested that Scott move them. He did so, efficiently this time.

Bill and Claire started in on the second batch of ten but he was no longer focused. He kept glancing over at the counter and finally she followed his gaze. One carrot in the pile that Scott had prepared was sticking out a full inch from the rest. Claire led Bill to the pile and said mildly, "Do you want to fix it, Bill?" Bill spent the next full minute adjusting the carrots into a uniform pile and then returned willingly to the stack of unpeeled carrots waiting to be dealt with. But Daisuke threw down his spoon and called out to Scott, "I'd like to see you outside for a minute—now."

Claire did not know what was said between the two men, but the rest of the morning went smoothly. There were no more incidents and Scott even stopped the irritating humming he'd been doing that Bill had clearly found distracting. By the eleven o'clock deadline, all 50 carrots were peeled washed and chopped, and Bill watched as Daisuke ceremoniously added them to the soup base he'd prepared. Then Bill went out to have his *coffee break* under the watchful eye of Susie, the day server, and Claire returned to the cash desk to see how Roscoe was doing.

While working on the carrots, Claire had mentally speculated about what Daisuke might have said outside. What Scott did not realize was how close Daisuke was to Roscoe. Roscoe, who always saw the good in everybody and was always concerned for the people around him to be happy, most certainly would have talked to Daisuke about Bill when he heard that Bill was to work in *The Three Musketeers* kitchen. Roscoe was very perceptive in his own way. He'd met Scott and likely had his own concerns. He probably didn't say anything bad about him to Daisuke. That was not

Roscoe's way. But he would have told Daisuke about the sorts of things that caused Bill to become agitated.

Claire grinned to herself about how the morning had gone as she approached the cash desk. It was so great to be working together as part of a team, a team of people who cared about each other and helped each other out. This was the real guts behind community living.

Chapter 45: Roscoe Cashes—and It *Was* a Good Day Until....

Roscoe was looking very pleased with himself when Claire greeted Mandy and him at the cash desk. "I cash, Claih! I cash for Ella myseff!"

Claire looked questioningly at Mandy and she explained, "Roscoe was watching me closely all morning. When Ella came in from next door—she runs the Laundromat and she knows Roscoe—and ordered a cup of coffee to go, he asked if he could cash her order. And he did it right except for one little glitch! I showed him the cancel button and how to correct it and then he finished her bill. Ella was very impressed!"

"But I still took longah dan Mandy—so I give Ella a piece of coco cweam pie onna house. And she was happy!"

"Wow!" Claire exclaimed. "Congratulations! I didn't think you'd learn so fast!" She looked at Mandy, willing her to say something more.

"I figure since Roscoe's going to be here three mornings a week now he might as well take over the coffee orders to give me a break," Mandy told Claire. "But no more free pie, Roscoe! If people don't want to wait a few extra seconds, you can just tell them to go elsewhere. It *is* your restaurant now so you can call the shots!"

Roscoe turned to Claire. "But I like people to be happy!"

"It's okay sometimes, Roscoe, but Mandy's right. You're trying to run a business here so you can't be giving away free food to everybody! Remember, you said you were going to use your profits to give the staff a raise—and also you were going to pay for Bill and Mavis to go with you on a holiday to Mexico again next March? If you keep giving away free pie, you won't have enough money left over!"

"Oh-h-h, I see," Roscoe replied thoughtfully.

Claire could see that he was mulling over what she'd said, probably trying to find a way to please everybody. She thought again about what a nice person Roscoe was. Then her thoughts wandered to Mandy. She had no special *disabilities training*. Yet she'd instinctively known not to use words like *just* and *simple* when she explained about Roscoe doing the future coffee orders.

Claire had fallen into that trap herself at times and then watched the play of emotions across Roscoe's face as at first he heard the compliment—that he was capable of doing something—and then registered the rider—but only if it was really easy. Claire ruminated to herself about how many nice, decent, socially sensitive people there were in the world despite all the horrible things that kept happening. But just then, the phone rang and her happy mental wanderings were brought to an abrupt halt.

Chapter 46: It Had to Happen!

Claire picked up the phone, noting with a frisson of dread that the call was coming from the school. "Claire? It's Doreen. We need you to come and pick up Jessie. Nico was hit by a car! He's on the way to the hospital and the police are here now. They want to interview Bertha and there's nobody to care for Jessie––and everything is upside down anyway. Please hurry!"

Claire gasped and thought rapidly. "I'm at the restaurant with Bill and Roscoe, but I'm driving the wheelchair van. I'll come right away but I need you to bring Jessie out so I don't have to leave Bill and Roscoe alone in the van. Can you do that?"

"I think so," Doreen agreed. "But please hurry!"

"I'll be there in five minutes. Just watch for me. I'll pull up right in front!"

Later, seven of them sat stunned, ringed around the dining room table at Bill and Roscoe's house with no way to get information and nothing to do but speculate. Tia was there and Gus and Amanda had come as soon as their lunchroom duties were over. Doreen hadn't answered their phone messages, Bertha was unavailable, and Claire did not dare call Angela. Gustaf was at a previously arranged principals' meeting downtown.

"We heard brakes squealing and then we heard people yelling but we never *saw* anything," Amanda said.

"The windows in the lunchroom downstairs don't face the street," Gus explained. "I ran up to see what was happening, but I couldn't even get close enough to him to see how badly he was hurt."

"I was watching a local cooking show on TV and they interrupted it with a breaking news bulletin," Tia added. "They said a student had been *seriously injured*!"

Roscoe and Bill looked glum. This should have been a happy visit for them. They should all have been talking about their successful ventures at the restaurant. Instead, this horrible thing had happened. "Nik-Nik okay?" Bill asked fearfully.

"I don't know, Bill," Claire replied sombrely.

"We could visit him. Take flowahs?" Roscoe suggested.

"I don't think he can have visitors right now, Roscoe," Claire replied sadly. "We just have to wait and see what happens." And then she added with a small sob in her voice, "It's really hard to wait when you don't know what's going to happen, isn't it?" Roscoe patted her awkwardly on the shoulder.

"Try Doreen again," Gus suggested. "She *has* to answer the phone sooner or later!" And this time, Doreen did.

"Angela just called," Doreen said abruptly, having registered who it was from the call display. "She said she's suing the school! Nico has a broken leg and he chipped his front tooth when his face slammed against the pavement. But he was conscious when the ambulance arrived so that's a good sign. The doctors are still checking for internal injuries and once he's stabilized, they are going to sedate him so he can have a CT scan to see if there's any brain swelling."

"Thank God it's not worse than that!" Claire replied, and everyone around the table, even Jessie, nodded their heads. Claire had put the phone on speaker.

Doreen put them on hold while she took another call. When she came back, she said, "Gustaf just heard and he's on his way back so I can't talk long."

Claire responded, "I'm sure it wasn't Bertha's fault––and it's not the school's fault. It was a board decision to put Nico and Jessie together with one assistant and Angela was right to be concerned about that. I have been, too. It just didn't make any sense. Tell Gustaf..."

"Gotta go. Here he comes!" and with that Doreen hung up the phone.

The next day, Claire had the opportunity to talk to Bertha, who was feeling very badly over what had happened. She told Claire that she'd been putting Jessie on her commode when Nico took the opportunity to run away. He was actually in the classroom with the teacher, but Alana had been writing on the blackboard at the time. Some of the other students had been horsing around and nobody noticed Nico slip out the door. It was not until Bertha returned to the classroom that anyone was even aware that he was gone, and it was just at that moment that they heard the squeal of brakes and a scream.

Because of the earlier murder, the school had been flagged and Inspector McCoy had been notified of the accident. Bertha told Claire that he and Sergeant Crombie had been out to interview her shortly after the accident happened. Then Sergeant Crombie had gone on to the hospital in the hope of meeting up with Nico's parents. He had been kind enough to phone Bertha back and update her since he had seen how upset she was.

Angela wanted to sue everybody, including John Baer, the poor man whose car had hit Nico, through absolutely no fault of his own according to several witnesses. Nico had run right out in front of the car. Baer had slammed on the brakes and swerved the car violently to the left, ramming it hard into the concrete median. The car had taken the brunt of the impact, but Nico had still been tossed a couple of feet. Unfortunately, he'd fallen face down, his leg landing awkwardly across the median, and that's what had caused the worst damage. But the CT scan had showed no sign of significant brain swelling and the doctors believed that Nico luckily had sustained only a mild concussion. The dentist thought he could save the front tooth. But the orthopaedic surgeon had informed Nico's parents that he'd sustained a transverse fracture of the distal femur in his left leg. He would need to remain in the hospital with his leg restrained in a sling for a week until the swelling went down enough so the fracture team could see exactly what they were dealing with before they casted it. However, so far it looked like a clean break and the bone had not punctured the skin. They were optimistic that with careful casting and no weight bearing for at least six weeks Nico would eventually get back the full use of his leg. But given the fact that he was not able to understand and cooperate with the treatment regimen, he'd need to go into the rehabilitation hospital once the active treatment phase of his recovery was over. It wouldn't be safe for him to leave there and return to school until well into the new year—possibly February.

All this, Bertha repeated faithfully to Claire, Gustaf, Alana and anyone else at the school who was interested. None of them were contacted directly by Nico's parents but, in due course, a letter arrived from a lawyer stating that a civil suit against the school was proceeding. That, compounded by the fact that a police investigation of the microwave incident had indicated active sabotage and the Health and Safety Inspection report indicated substandard installation of the microwave to begin with, had principal Gustaf Lennon in a chronically fearful state, worried that he'd now have two lawsuits on his hands.

Claire sent flowers to Nico's home and the school sent a get-well card signed by Bertha, Alana, Gustaf and all the students in Nico's class, along with a huge stuffed giraffe to the hospital. There was no acknowledgement of either offering. School continued as normal with Bertha working only with Jessie now. Gustaf tentatively suggested that, since Bertha had been hired to work half-time with Jessie and half-time with Nico, that Claire should keep Jessie home in the afternoons so Bertha could be freed up to work with other students with learning problems. However, Claire adamantly refused to consider this idea and Gustaf did not pursue the issue further.

Chapter 47: A Stalled Investigation

A few days later, Claire stopped by the school for one of her visits with Jessie, mostly to see how she and Bertha were relating now that Bertha's attention was no longer being divided. While saying hello to Doreen, she noticed that Gustaf was sitting in his office with the door slightly open. Claire knocked tentatively and he invited her in. After the usual civilities, Claire broached the subject of the lawsuit, which was common gossip around the school.

"It's not my liability!" he said. Gustaf turned and rummaged through the files in his desk before triumphantly pulling out a letter that he handed to Claire. She noted the date, July 15th, and quickly scanned it. Gustaf had just been informed at that time of the upcoming placement of Jessie and Nico together in his school with one assistant. He was writing to object on the grounds that their needs were too different and that they could not safely be worked with together with one assistant. The response from the board was attached, indicating that this was how it had to be because of financial constraints and the fact that the learning experts at the central office thought it would be okay. "You see!" he crowed. "She can't sue *me*."

Claire looked at him sadly, feeling a sudden empathy for Angela. Gustaf would always come first for Gustaf, far ahead of the students for whom he was responsible. *He'd have acted exactly the same if it had been Jessie who'd been hurt rather than Nico*, she thought.

"What about the microwave?" she asked. "What's happening there?"

"I don't know yet, but again I'm not responsible. That microwave was installed long before I came to the school. Even the board that was put on the front of it happened before my time. I have no reason to go into that room and can't be expected to know the idiosyncrasies of every single appliance in this school!"

Claire left Gustaf's office with a bad taste in her mouth. She decided that she didn't like him very much and that the school board would be better off without administrators like him. She was very soon to regret those uncharitable thoughts.

It was now the third week in November. The snow was there to stay and the countdown to Christmas had begun. But there was still no break in the case. *On a positive note,* Claire thought, *Jessie and Bertha had formed a solid relationship.* With the time to focus solely on Jessie, Bertha had learned to read Jessie's nonverbal cues and Jessie had learned to see past Bertha's rather abrupt manner to the basically good person underneath. On a negative note, Nico's recovery had been slowed by an infection in his leg, and the civil case for negligence against the school board, the school, Gustaf, Alana and Bertha was proceeding with a hearing expected in early January.

Claire woke up one morning, deciding that enough was enough and she made a number of phone calls to gather the troops for a strategy meeting. Bill was away at his day program, which he still attended on the two days a week when he was not at the restaurant. This was an at-home morning for Roscoe, and he was invited to join the rest of them in their planning session.

Gus and Amanda were the first to arrive, and Amanda plunked down copies of her assigned project for each of them. Gus sniffed. Tia trailed in ten minutes after the agreed upon 9:30 time. She patted her belly that was beginning to plump out and declared that mornings were no longer the best time for her.

Chapter 48: The Primary Suspects

Amanda was the first to speak. "As you know," she said, "I asked Doreen to do the questioning of Bruce, the UPS man, since she'd already met him a few times." Gus chose that moment to clear her throat but said nothing further. "Here's what Doreen discovered," Amanda continued, and began reading from Doreen's written report.

"Bruce delivered packages to the office on November 12th and November 17th. On both occasions, I was able to take him to the staff room for coffee and a visit, and he was quite happy to talk rather than keep working. And he particularly likes to talk about himself!

"We were fortunate to find the staff room empty both times and I gradually brought the conversation around to the topic of Pamela and watched him closely. He did comment that she was a pretty girl, but he actually spent a lot more time discussing an assistant that he'd met recently at another school where he delivers. He said that, unlike Pamela, she was single and seemed interested in him. He was planning to ask her out soon, just trying to get up his courage. He asked me if I had any suggestions for how to broach the topic.

"I couldn't get much more out of him of any use to our investigation. But I honestly don't think he's the type to push Pamela over the rail. I don't think he had a motive. He doesn't come across as angry or sad or moping about anyone or anything and seems to have moved on quite readily to another girl. Also, his blue delivery uniform stands out quite clearly and somebody would have been bound to have noticed it up there after Pamela fell. Also, I checked back through the pile of delivery slips and there's no record of a delivery the day Pamela fell."

Amanda finished reading and placed Doreen's report face down on the table. Claire sighed and said, "I think Doreen is right and we should just forget about him."

The others murmured in agreement.

Gus went next and cleared her throat in a ponderous kind of way. Claire, knowing that posture of her aunt's, looked at her watch ostentatiously, and warned Gus to be as brief as possible since they had to cover all the suspects in an hour. Gus looked a bit crestfallen but then squared her shoulders and began. 'I have sat in Brian's drama class with Jessie eight times now. I have the following observations to make." Gus consulted her page of notes at this point.

"The students seem to like him, but I'm not sure how much they respect him. I have overheard a couple of them refer to him as a nerd, although he does seem to have good class control. He prepares well and everyone seems to find his classroom presentations interesting. I know *I* do. Jessie also seems to enjoy the class, especially when he role plays certain parts."

Gus thought for a minute and then went on, "It's hard to sit there and try to figure out somebody's secret thoughts just from what they say, but what has been most helpful are remarks from some of the students." Here, she consulted her notes again and then went on, "As we agreed, I have never mentioned Pamela, but a couple of the students actually brought her death up with me at break time. I did ask them if they were frightened being in a school where a murder had occurred and if they'd ever wondered if the murderer was still around. They didn't seem worried about that."

After an additional pause, Gus went on, speaking rather slowly and dramatically. Claire suspected she had already forgotten about the time constraint and shuffled her feet impatiently. Gus took the hint and spoke more quickly, "One day, a woman came to the door and handed one of the students at the back a folded note to be given to Brian. He stood at the front of the class, looked from side to side, opened the note, studied it carefully with kind of a frown on his face and then he read it out loud."

"What did it say?" Claire asked. She noted that Amanda's lips were pinched together as if this was something she already knew, but had promised to keep secret. Clearly, this was to be Gus' big moment and there was no hurrying her.

"It sa-a-i-d .... 'Please pick up one dozen eggs, two litres of milk and one loaf of whole wheat bread'." By the look on Gus' face, it was clear that Gus had noticed that her audience was beginning to look vexed at this point and she hastened to enlighten them. "Brian had chosen this way to let his students be the first to know that he'd married a French teacher named Francine Cloutier from the Roman Catholic school a block over. He made the whole thing very dramatic and incorporated it into the lesson he was teaching for the day on the value of props and dramatic pauses when acting.

"Clever! Do you have any idea when he got involved with her?" Tia asked.

"Yes. At break time, Jessie and I congratulated him and I casually asked him that very question. He said he met her a few weeks into the school year and was attracted to her from the beginning. He *volunteered*, however, that he'd been initially quite drawn to Pamela as well, not realizing that she was married since she did not wear a ring. But one day, Francine was visiting the school because she'd been invited to co-teach a class and afterwards, she happened to see Brian and Pamela flirting back and forth. Francine thought it was serious and started to walk away and that was when Brian realized that he had to have her in his life. He actually told me that he stopped flirting with Pamela after that and even told her about Francine, but she didn't take kindly to this change in him and became quite cool whenever their paths crossed.

"That explains what Doreen told us about the change in the way they related to one another," Claire commented.

"Wow! What a story! I guess we can cross him off our list," Tia added, and Claire, Gus and Amanda nodded in agreement.

Chapter 49: The Secondary Suspects

Although the two school consultants had never been very likely prospects, they had to be considered too. "I'll go next," Claire said, and she briefly related the exchange she'd had with Gerald Kuhn, the reading specialist. "I really don't think he could have done it. He talked quite openly about liking her and being attracted to her. He knew she was married and respected that boundary from what he said. His big regret was that he'd not had time to talk to her the last time he saw her before she died.

"I checked with Doreen and she confirmed that he wasn't scheduled to be in the school that day, and nobody reported seeing him. According to Doreen, all the staff has been very quick to compare notes on who they saw at the time of the murder. If he *had* been in the school, somebody would have mentioned it to Doreen since it was the natural topic of conversation for weeks after it happened."

"Well, that just leaves Richard Dawson," Tia said. "He was *my* project, if you recall. I did try to track him down, but Doreen informed me that he was no longer coming to the school and a new speech and language pathologist had replaced him a couple of weeks after Pamela's death. That sounded very suspicious and I had no real way of checking, so I borrowed a note out of Amanda's book and got Doreen to do it." Gus chortled at this and Amanda winced.

"Doreen checked with a friend in personnel at Central Office and found out that Richard was on extended sick leave and had terminal cancer. According to Doreen's friend, he'd been sick for some time but tried to keep going. He often missed work and there had been complaints coming in about incomplete reports. He was pretty frail, down to about 120 pounds apparently, and the gossip is that he was more or less asked to go on leave rather than be terminated. The last time he was in the school that anybody can remember is about a week before Pamela died."

"So I guess he's out," Gus commented, "and it sounds like we're out of suspects."

"Not quite," Tia said quietly.

That got everyone's attention and Tia went on. "For a while now, Claire has been talking about scouting out restaurants near the school where Pamela might have liaised with someone at lunchtime. It didn't seem very likely to me, given her schedule, but since I'd struck out with Richard very quickly, I thought I'd put my unused energies into following up that lead. With Doreen's help, I managed to get individual pictures of the two consultants and the deliveryman, but for some reason there was no picture available of Brian Littner. Finally, she gave me a copy of a group staff photo and I had to use that.

"I started with the restaurants nearest the school and reasoned that if these meetings existed they'd be clandestine and, if so, Pamela and her paramour would choose some tiny place that could not accommodate large groups. I went around to three or four places and was about to give up and broaden the search radius when I spotted a tiny hole-in-the-wall kind of place on a back street, two blocks over from the school. It actually looked kind of dicey and I wasn't sure what kind of reception I'd get.

"The inside was cleaner and brighter than the outside would have suggested. The proprietor or manager or whoever he was appeared to be Italian and all the signs were in Italian. He looked like a decent guy and I decided that I'd just be honest with what we wanted and why. I spoke to him in Italian and he seemed pleased. I asked him where he was from and it turns out it was a small town near where my parents came from so I lapsed into dialect and he did the same. This allowed us to talk privately because even the few Italians who were in there were unlikely to speak our particular dialect. He told me that he'd met nobody else here from his area of Italy and seemed eager to oblige me.

"I showed him all the pictures and pointed to Brian in the group picture, but he just shook his head. I asked him to please look again and I must have looked very disappointed, which I was, because he studied the picture for a long time. His finger kept waving around over the faces and finally he settled on one. I couldn't believe it and he admitted he wasn't sure. So I went back to the school and got some more pictures of that individual who was *not* Brian.

"This time he identified him for sure. According to him, this man and Pamela only came in together at lunchtime once, but they had come in after school, around four, on five or six different occasions. The man in question had slipped him a twenty each time and he let them use a back room where he apparently served selected people drinks. He's not licensed and was very anxious that we not tell the police."

"Well, who was he?" Gus asked impatiently.

"The principal, Gustaf!"

Claire looked stunned. "When did you find this out, Tia, and when were you going to tell me if I hadn't arranged this meeting?"

Tia looked at her friend defensively. "I actually only found out the day before yesterday. I was going to tell you when you called, but we did keep talking about working as a team so I thought I could wait until this meeting."

Claire just shook her head but what she was thinking was *It's happening already, the pregnancy, the distancing!*

Amanda broke into her thoughts. "What are we going to do now? He could be the killer and we're around him every day!"

"I'll deal with him," Claire said. "I'll get his address from Doreen and visit him at home. Maybe they were having an affair, but it doesn't mean he killed her. Maybe we have to take a second look at the husband after all."

"You can't go there on your own!" Gus blustered. "I'll tell Dan."

"I *am* going," Claire retorted, "but don't worry. I'm not going to take Jessie."

Nobody could miss the cold sarcasm in her tone and the three of them looked at her in surprise. It was not like Claire, who was a team player if anybody was. She went on, "And if you mention this to Dan, Aunt Gus, I will *not* forgive you."

Claire's voice held a menacing edge and even Claire didn't know where it came from. But the stricken look on her face suggested that Tia did. And the very fact that Gus remained silent, indicated that she also knew. Only Amanda was having a hard time understanding Claire's peculiar reaction.

People who are not well loved cannot trust at a very deep level. Claire felt betrayed by Tia, and now she was feeling bitter and isolated and that it was all up to her. It was a tiny step for her to go to feeling worthless, abandoned, alone—feelings that had been very familiar to her throughout her younger years. All that seemed to matter in her own mind right now was that she solve this murder, whatever the cost. Her own well being was not a significant factor to her at that moment.

Claire turned to Tia then and, in a cold voice, said, "I'd like the address of that Italian bistro or whatever it is, please, and also the name of the proprietor."

Chapter 50: Three Different Lives; Three Different Projects

The next day was Wednesday and Roscoe and Bill were scheduled to go to the restaurant in the morning to work. At this point, Satou was coming in two mornings a week to work with Bill. He'd started out coming in one day when Bill began working there and had immediately recognized Bill's strong focus and fascination with the knife. They had begun working together wordlessly through Satou's demonstrations and through the video clips he'd saved from his work as a master chef in Japan. Communication had not turned out to be an issue.

From the loving and intimate way in which Satou handled the knives, Claire was beginning to suspect that here was another soul on the autism spectrum, albeit at the high end. It was wonderful to see Bill's response and Satou's joy in finding someone to share his relationship with the knife with. Each filled a need in the other.

Satou had juggled his knives once in front of Bill and Bill had been fascinated. But Claire asked him not to do it again. She was afraid Bill would try to copy Satou and get hurt. Bill could actually dice very fast now. He had formed his own relationship with the knife and it was a very tight bond. Claire just hoped that Bill's Social Worker would not come in when he was in the midst of one of his artful, wild prep sessions. She might consider Claire very irresponsible and institute some sort of limits.

Roscoe plodded away patiently at the cash register. Unlike Bill, he was a people person. There were mistakes; sometimes people took advantage of him— but more often they helped him. Everybody liked Roscoe. They could not help themselves. His smile; his innocent look; his trust; his genuine interest and concern for others.

Meanwhile, back at the school, Gustaf was exacting his own revenge on Angela for her lawsuit, albeit in a highly professional and appropriate manner. He dictated the following letter to Doreen who surreptitiously made a copy of it for the group and handed it off to Amanda in a sealed envelope when she saw her alone at lunch one day. The body of the letter read as follows:

"Dear Mr. and Mrs. Arietti:

"This letter is to inform you that we are no longer able to provide an appropriate level of service for your son, Nico. We have referred him to the board's behaviour management class for children 9 to 14 who, due to their uncontrollable behaviour, are at risk to themselves or others and require a higher level of supervision than can be provided in regular classrooms. Ms. Sheila Willis, the coordinator in charge of the board's special needs classrooms, will be in touch with you closer to the time for Nico to join the class. If you would like to meet with her before then, I am attaching the contact information.

"I am sure you will find this class to be a good and appropriate setting for Nico that will give him the opportunity to advance his academic skills without all the attention that can be given to him diverted into controlling his behaviours. You will also meet other parents struggling with similar issues and will find that the parents in this class have formed a powerful support group that you may want to join.

"We wish you the best of luck with Nico's future academic progress and hope that he will make a complete recovery from his recent accident."

Chapter 51:   The Good Side of Angela; the Sneaky Side of Claire

Two days later, there was another group meeting at Roscoe's home in the afternoon. Claire and Gus chortled with glee when Amanda read the letter from Gustaf to Angela, but Tia did not see it that way.

"You know, when you think about it, Angela has only been trying to do the best she knows for Nico, just as you're trying to do for Jessie, Claire. And she has bought into this integration business just like you, so this letter must have been very painful for her."

"Well, she shouldn't have been so mean and bull-headed then and it might not have come to this!"

"She may be very opinionated in some ways, but then so are you. She may not have the right answers but she clearly believes that she does. And you yourself have said how hard it must be to live with a child like Nico. Caring for him must be much harder than caring for Jessie in some ways."

"Come *on,* Tia! Caring for Jessie is much more demanding. She can't do *anything* for herself!" Gus retorted.

"Yes, I know, Gus—but she also can't run away or break things or throw things or put her own life in danger through her actions. And she's grateful for what you do for her, not sneaky and defiant like Nico can be, according to what you've told me yourself, Claire!"

"Yes, you have a point, Tia, and I shouldn't have laughed. Angela and Paolo really are in a difficult position. But in the final analysis, I honestly do think this will be a better placement for Nico and that's more important than Angela's hurt feelings."

"I grant you that," Tia replied, "but let's just not gloat over it."

The meeting broke up shortly after that. There was nothing more to say, as Claire had not yet had the opportunity to visit Gustaf. However, she had visited the little restaurant where he and Pamela had reportedly met and had talked to the owner, Enrico, who told her essentially the same story he'd told to Tia. Claire was now very anxious to proceed with the visit to Gustaf's home and, once she was alone, she phoned a part-time staff member, Stacey Williams, and asked her to come in and work with Roscoe from 11:30 to 4:30 the next day.

When Stacey arrived the next morning, Claire went quickly through the program she'd outlined for Roscoe to follow and then left for the school. She lurked a discreet distance from the office door and waited for Gustaf to leave, which he did at 11:55.

Claire had already checked the phone listings for Gustaf's address but it was not listed. Her hope now was that she could convince Doreen to give it to her. But Doreen was not willing to give her Gustaf's address "He'll know it came from me and I'll lose my job," she said.

Claire took a deep breath and decided she'd have to tell Doreen what she'd found out about the relationship between Pamela and Gustaf and then swear her to secrecy. Doreen was shocked and disbelieving. "I saw them relating lots of times and there was no sign of anything more. I still can't give you the info but you could try the land titles office. I happen to know that he bought a house in the Pleasantview area near the school last year. He likes to ride his bicycle back and forth. He's quite interested in fitness."

Claire's immediate thought was to turn to Tia for help, but she didn't want to do that now. Gus and Amanda were still in the lunchroom and she went downstairs to talk to them, very quietly so as not to be overheard. Amanda had become quite a computer aficionado. Gus often sneered at her new hobby, but the sneer covered up her own feelings of insecurity. Gus felt at a loss with technological matters and avoided the new technology as much as possible.

Amanda advised Claire to go home or to Roscoe's house and said she'd email her as soon as she had information. Amanda always brought her laptop with her and worked away on it during lunch hours while Gus read a book. After Claire left, Amanda connected to the school's Wi-Fi and searched for new house purchases in the Pleasantview area of Edmonton over the past 18 months. She found six listings. Since she didn't have immediate access to a printer, she pasted the file into a word document that she stored on her desktop. Then she pulled up the reverse phone directory, entered in each of the addresses and got the phone numbers that matched them. She emailed the list to Claire and told her that was all she could do.

All this time, Gus was tut-tutting at her sententiously, saying Amanda should not help Claire with this. It was dangerous and what would Dan say? Amanda ignored her, only responding that where there's a will, there's a way and, if she didn't help, Claire would find out anyway.

Claire *did* go home. She had only one focus and no appetite for working with Roscoe anymore that day. When she received the list, she systematically phoned all six addresses and was able to eliminate three of them immediately because someone was home during the day to answer the phone. She studied the descriptions of the remaining three and saw that one of them was huge, almost 4000 square feet on three levels with a walkout basement. She doubted that Gustaf would want to maintain a home like that or would have any use for all that space since, to the best of her knowledge, he lived alone.

Claire always liked action best and, after thinking for a minute, she left her house, jumped in her car and headed off to the first address. Maybe she could go by those houses and check the mailboxes. If nobody was home, the chances were that the mail was still there. She did just that and at the second house, she finally found what she was looking for—a utility bill addressed to Mr. Gustaf Lennon! Claire quickly returned to her car, wrote down the address and went home.

When Karen arrived for the after school care, Claire informed her that she needed to go out that evening and asked if Karen could stay until nine instead of eight and get Jessie all ready for bed before she left. She then informed Dan that she'd arranged a meeting with a family struggling to provide care for their adopted daughter, recently diagnosed with spastic quadriplegia. He raised his eyebrows signalling that here she was again trying to save the world but said nothing. Claire left, feeling only a little guilty over this latest deception.

Chapter 52: The Confrontation with Gustaf

When Claire arrived at Gustaf's home, she noted with satisfaction that his car was in the driveway. There was another car parked in front that looked vaguely familiar—a black Fiat 500 Turbo—but it was a common enough car. Maybe it belonged to a neighbour's visitor.

Claire rang the doorbell, but there was no answer. She rang again and stood there waiting. Eventually, she heard shuffling sounds from inside and the front door opened. Gustaf stood there, a whiskey glass in his hand, looking a bit bleary eyed.

He blinked in recognition and then asked, "What are *you* doing here?"

"I need to talk to you about something that couldn't be discussed at school," Claire said simply.

Gustaf hesitated but then opened the door wider. "You better come in, I suppose," he said, not too hospitably.

Claire sat down in a beige armchair near the door and he perched on a nearby sofa. "Yes?" he asked in a clipped tone.

"I *know* you were seeing Pamela before she died. What I *want* to know is if that had anything to do with her murder?"

Gustaf stared at her in surprise. "How...?"

"It doesn't matter—but it didn't come from anybody at school. As far as I'm aware, nobody else knows and I plan to keep it that way unless it's directly relevant to the murder investigation. I have no desire to jeopardize

Jessie's placement nor to cause you any unnecessary embarrassment."

Gustaf gave her a measured look and Claire had her first qualm. *Why hadn't she just gone all the way and told him that nobody knew she was there and he could do anything he wanted to her with no one being the wiser.* Not for the first time, she realized how her obsessive thirst for answers could cause her brain to suddenly stop working. But then she remembered that she had good instincts. Her bravado in coming here had been based on knowledge of Gustaf's character acquired through their more than a dozen interactions to date. Gustaf was fearful, he was calculating, and he was on the lazy side and liked easy answers. Throwing Pamela over the school railing didn't fit with this picture of his character.

Claire looked at him and said softly, "I just want to know whatever you can tell me about Pamela, Gustaf— so I can go ahead and find the murderer and we can all get on with our lives." He looked at her doubtfully and she added, "I've solved or *helped* to solve several murders already. I seem to have a knack for it. Please help me out here."

Gustaf didn't answer directly, but instead asked if he could get her a drink. Claire took that to mean that he'd like another himself, but didn't feel comfortable drinking alone in front of her. "Okay, thanks," she responded. "Do you happen to have any lite beer?"

Gustaf went to the kitchen and returned with an opened bottle of Coors and a glass. "You're in luck. I keep these on hand for my exercise days!" he commented, in a more relaxed tone than he'd used before.

Claire thanked him and he sat down, took a generous swallow of his refreshed whiskey and began, "It's true that Pamela and I had a little fling. We just enjoyed each other's company, but knew it couldn't go anywhere." Claire, always one to push the envelope, raised her eyebrows.

"Fine!" he said. "I was attracted by her looks and her easy manner. She was intrigued by my position and probably by my reputation for elusiveness and keeping a professional distance."

Claire had the grace to blush, remembering her gossip session with Doreen. If Gustaf noticed, he didn't let on and continued his story.

"Pamela liked a challenge and she was obviously used to using her looks and her wiles to get what she wanted."

That's right, Claire thought. *Blame the dead woman!* But she wasn't here to judge, she reminded herself. "Go on," she said mildly.

"Pamela told me that her husband was just a dumb working Joe with no ambition and she was tired of him. She wanted to get ahead, join the professional ranks, maybe become a teacher or consultant. And she wanted me to help her—call in some favors or pull some strings. I knew there wasn't much I could do for her, but I offered to call some people, not that I planned to. It would have been *very* unprofessional! But like I said, we were having a nice little fling."

Claire worked hard to keep her face neutral. *I'm not here to judge!* she reminded herself again. Instead, she asked, "Did Pamela ever mention anything about anyone threatening her? I heard that her husband turned up at the school a couple of times and was quite abusive."

"Oh, she was annoyed about that. Said he was just a big oaf who liked to act tough in front of others. Said she couldn't wait to get rid of him, but right then she couldn't afford to live on her own. I sidestepped that conversation because I knew where it was heading."

Again, Claire swallowed her disgust and asked instead, "Did she say if he'd ever hit her? Somebody at school mentioned seeing bruises on her arms a couple of times."

"Hah! You should have seen the bruises on her legs!"

Claire squirmed but only said, "She was always wearing pants whenever I saw her."

"She was a kick boxer!" Gustaf announced, with what seemed to Claire to be a misplaced sense of pride. "She even won some competitions!" After a pause, *undoubtedly for effect*, Claire thought, Gustaf went on. "Pam could definitely look after herself but from what she told, me her husband was a wuss!"

"Well, she wasn't looking after herself when somebody threw her over the balcony," Claire commented.

"Whoever that was, they must have caught her by surprise."

Claire tried another tack. "You said she couldn't afford to leave her husband, but she always dressed pretty nicely. Was *he* providing her all the money for those high-end clothes?"

"Pam never discussed her finances with me directly, but she did comment once that she had her ways of getting by, whatever *that* meant."

Claire wondered if it meant blackmail—or if it meant other secret relationships. "Gustaf, I heard from somebody that she'd received a threatening letter. Did she ever mention that to you?"

"No-o," he said. "But I *do* remember one time when she seemed kind of down. I asked her what was the matter but she just brushed it off."

"Do you remember when that was?"

Gustaf thought for a minute and then replied, "I think it would have been the first week of October. I seem to remember that it was picture-taking day."

"That fits with the timeline I heard," Claire said. She was silent for a minute and then added, "Can you think of anything else—anything else at all—that might help to identify the killer? Were there any other odd things that happened during your time with her?"

Gustaf thought for a minute and then said, "No-o, nothing comes to mind." After a pause he added, "I hope you find the killer, Claire. Pam may have been a little on the wild side, but she didn't deserve that!" Claire thought about the pot calling the kettle black and then sadly recalled how Tia used to jibe her about her endless supply of clichés.

Gustaf stood up and spoke again when she didn't answer. "I trust there will be no need to air Pam's dirty linen in public?" he asked.

Again! Claire thought. *Surely it took two people to dirty this kind of linen!* But she said only, "I want to thank you very much for being so frank with me, Gustaf—and I promise I will not be discussing our meeting with anyone who could possibly harm the reputation of you or Pamela. I don't really know where to go from here, but I think, despite everything Pamela thought about her husband, I *will* need to consider him. If he'd found out about the two of you, he could very well have become angry enough to kill her, even if that level of violence was not normally part of his character. Apart from that, we're basically at a dead end and I think the police are in the same place."

"You will keep me informed?" Gustaf asked nervously. "If he really was that angry, he might come after me, too."

"I promise," Claire said soberly. "And thank you, again!" She said her good-byes and stepped out into the cold November night. It was quite dark and already twenty minutes to ten. Dan would be wondering where she was.

As Claire approached her car, she noted that the car she'd seen earlier was still there and just for a second, she thought she saw a shadow inside. *Must be my imagination,* she thought. But she unlocked her own car door, quickly slid inside and relocked the door. There *was* a murderer out there somewhere and she was pretty sure it was not Gustaf.

Chapter 53: Another Tragedy; Another Mystery

The next day, a Thursday, was a day program day for Bill, and Claire was at Roscoe's home working on his math. For every ten exercises he got right, they played a game of Blokus, a spatial reasoning game that challenged both of them and they both looked forward to those games. At 11:05, the phone rang and Claire noted from the display that it was the school number. She felt the familiar tension; had something happened to Jessie?

"Hello, Claire. It's Doreen," came the almost inaudible whisper over the phone.

"What's wrong?" Claire asked, anxiety sharpening her voice.

"Did you every find Gustaf's address and did you visit him last night?"

Claire hesitated for a second, but couldn't see any harm in answering. "Yes and yes. Why?"

"Some time last night he was murdered!"

"Oh, my God! Oh!...O-o-h!" Claire exclaimed, as first shock and then the full implication of what she'd just admitted hit her. "Do they know when?"

"The coroner estimated some time between nine and eleven in the evening, based on body temperature and state of rigor mortis. Inspector McCoy and Sergeant Crombie were called to the scene, and the Sergeant was good enough to tell me when I asked." Doreen paused and then added, "I didn't tell him why I wanted to know, but I had a feeling *you*'d need to know."

"Doreen, don't say anything—please! I'll be over as soon as I can make arrangements for Roscoe," she said and hung up the phone abruptly. Her first thought was to phone Tia and she did so immediately. This was no time for grudges, real or imaginary. She quickly explained and asked Tia if she could work with Roscoe. "Bring him here," Tia said, "and bring that Blokus game. I'm dying to try it!"

Claire rushed to the school and into the office where Doreen was on the phone with Central Office. She held up a finger to Claire, listened carefully, and then hung up the phone. Then she took it off the hook, grabbed Claire, pulled her into Gustaf's office and closed the door. "Tell me!" she hissed. "What *happened?*" Claire told her everything as fast as she could while both of them nervously watched the clock. She'd just finished telling Doreen about the mystery car and warning her to repeat nothing to anyone, when they heard the chime in the outer office indicating the front door had opened. They quickly left Gustaf's office, and Claire scuttled out the door and down the hall towards Jessie's room while Doreen hung up the phone and sat down at her desk.

"Hello!" said the new arrival, "I'm Anne Rickles, assistant principal at St. Peter's. Central Office called and asked me to take over here for the time being. I'm sorry for your loss."

Doreen nodded her head numbly, gave her name and offered a perfunctory welcome.

"Was that Claire Burke I saw going down the hall just now?"

Doreen panicked momentarily, but managed to keep her face composed. "Why, yes!" she said, trying to strike a note of pleased surprise. "She's here to visit her daughter. She pops in quite often." After a short pause, she asked, "Do you know her?"

"Yes, of course! Jessie was at *our* school last year—in fact, for all of her elementary years. She was a real pleasure to work with according to the teachers and her former assistant. How is she getting on *here?*"

Doreen thought rapidly, but decided that the best strategy was to problematize in order to add credence to Claire's visit. "Not as well, I'm afraid. It's been a tough transition for her."

"I'm sorry to hear that. Well, maybe I'll catch up with Claire later, but right now we better get down to business. I understand that Central Office asked you to keep this information confidential for the time being. Have you done so?"

Doreen gulped and averred that she had. In fact, her concern had just been to tell Claire and she'd had no time to tell anyone else. And Claire wouldn't be talking!

Doreen showed Anne into Gustaf's office and soon the new substitute principal was busy on the phone. Doreen tried to focus on some deskwork awaiting her, but her head was roaring. She took two aspirin, and put her head in her hands. She raised it again shortly when she heard the chime for the front door, and a moment later Inspector McCoy and Sergeant Crombie were standing in front of her.

At his request, they moved into Gustaf's office and just as she closed the door, Doreen saw Claire slip by and out the door to her car. Anne and the three of them sat there while McCoy grilled Doreen on every single interaction she could remember that Gustaf had had in the past few days.

Doreen provided a rich abundance of extraneous detail, anything to keep him from remembering that his nemesis, Claire, often visited the school to see her daughter. Claire had told him how ready he was to make her a target. Unfortunately, she'd been one of the visitors that week and Doreen didn't dare exclude her name. But when she mentioned it, Anne said brightly "Oh! I saw her when I came in this morning—just heading down to her daughter's room, so if she's still here, you might be able to talk to her now." Turning to Doreen, she asked, "Can you call down to the room, Doreen, and find out?"

Doreen dutifully called, but ,of course, she knew what the answer would be. McCoy registered it, but didn't pursue it further. He had plenty of other people to focus on based on all the information Doreen had given him. Doreen returned to her desk then and was happy to see that McCoy had closed the door behind her. The first thing she did was to quietly send Claire a text message indicating that they needed to talk. Doreen felt that if she was going to protect Claire, she needed to know every detail of what had happened in her meeting with Gustaf the previous night so she could be absolutely convinced that Claire had nothing to do with his death.

Fortunately, Claire's phone dinged when she was with Tia because she'd returned there immediately after leaving the school. Claire looked at it helplessly, never having mastered the art of texting and Tia grabbed the phone in exasperation and decoded it for her. "What do you want me to text back to her?" Tia asked.

"Ask her if she can come here after school, please, and to call when she's on her way. Then call me at Roscoe's and I'll come over. Is that okay?" Claire added as an afterthought.

"Of course," Tia replied, and rapidly sent the message. In a moment, a positive reply came back.

Chapter 54: Will the *Real* Murderer Please Come Out?

Gustaf's funeral was held at St. Agnes' Church, near the school, and it was a very sad affair. His only family was his sister from Des Moines, Iowa, sitting in the front pew all by herself. Doreen had had a chance to talk to her when she came to the school to claim Gustaf's effects. She'd explained that Gustaf and she were the only children of their parents, now deceased. Their mother had been estranged from her two sisters and their father was an only child. All their grandparents were also now gone. Claudette was recently divorced from her husband of eighteen years and they'd had no children. She looked very small and frail sitting there alone.

Claire looked around her at those present. There were, of course, many teachers and other staff members from the school and, surprisingly, she noted that Thomas Abbott was also there. She saw a sprinkling of parents and students, but not as many as she might have expected. Gustaf was not the sort of man who endeared himself to people. Near the back, she saw Aunt Gus and Amanda sitting with Tia. They must have asked her to bring them. And just as the organ chords for the first hymn started, signalling the procession of the urn down the aisle, she saw Inspector McCoy and Sergeant Crombie slip in and take seats at opposite ends of the back row. They must be thinking that the killer might turn up.

The funeral service was short and to the point, mostly focusing on Gustaf's career as a teacher and school principal. The celebrant mentioned the sister and expressed his condolences. No burial service was announced, and following the service, the mourners convened in the reception hall in the basement where sandwiches, dessert bars, and tea and coffee were served. Claire joined Tia, Amanda and Aunt Gus, but they didn't plan to stay long. It was a depressing setting and it felt to Claire as if Gustaf had led a pretty empty life. She glanced out one of the windows that faced the parking lot and stiffened. "That's the kind of car I saw at Gustaf's place," she hissed to Tia, not wanting her aunt to hear. "I think I've just figured something out!" she added, as cold chills ran down her back. "I'm going to follow up on your lead, Tia!" and she turned on her heel and headed towards the door with Gus and Amanda staring after her.

Tia had a bad feeling. Her eyes followed Claire and she noted that Inspector McCoy and Sergeant Crombie were still in the room. She headed towards them.

Claire jumped in her car and headed back to the hole in the wall restaurant where Tia had first learned about Gustaf's affair with Pamela. She was, as usual, totally focused on her task and didn't notice that she was being followed. Enrico was there, Claire was relieved to see, and she headed over to him. He looked surprised to see her, but she wasted no time on preliminaries. "You mentioned that you had a cousin here, Enrico. Can you tell me his name?"

"*Her* name was like mine, Barcheballi, but she married a man from Rome, Paolo A..."

"Basta. Rico!" came a harsh voice from behind her.

"No, Angie!" was all Claire heard before the gun reverberated in her ear and Enrico slumped over the counter in front of her. She whirled to confront Angela Arietti!

"So you finally figured it out, you interfering bitch!" Angela snarled. "Well, it's not going to do you much good!"

Stall her; keep her talking! Claire thought to herself frantically. "Why did you do it, Angela? Why kill Pamela? She was doing everything you wanted with Nico. She hardly paid any attention to Jessie."

"And she never stopped talking about that, about how much Jessie responded and how much she needed those stupid exercises. She was *never* that interested in my Nico. I don't think she even *liked* him!" Claire saw a glitter in Angela's eye that could have been a tear but she didn't have time to observe too closely.

"But that's hardly..."

"Shut up! What do *you* know? She was obsessed with those gym workouts of hers and she became friends with a woman there, the daughter of someone who *used* to be a friend of mine. Not any more! Gina told Pamela that I *drank* when I was pregnant with Nico and Pamela wanted to tell the principal so she could get specialized help for Nico."

Claire knew that any second Angela would shoot her and that she'd probably last longer if she didn't respond, but she couldn't help herself. *At least, she could console herself that she'd finally solved the mystery—and without Tia's help!* she told herself triumphantly. Then she could have wept thinking of what harsh feelings she'd harboured for someone so important to her. All these thoughts flickered quickly through Claire's mind and then she became dimly aware that Angela was talking again.

"How did you know?" Angela screamed at her. "*Tell* me, before you die, bitch! I want to know!"

"I didn't," Claire said dully, realizing that her moments on this earth were numbered. "The car. I finally remembered it was like yours. And I remembered that Enrico was Italian and he mentioned a cousin. How else could you know about Pamela and Gustaf?"

"*What* about them? I don't know *anything* about them. What are you *talking* about?"

"Then why did you kill Gustaf?"

"That pig?" Angela sneered. "He kicked my Nico out—after what they *did* to him."

"But Gustaf didn't hit him. It was that John Baer who was driving the car. He had no connection with the school."

"It was *his* fault!" Angela fumed. "Nico should have had his *own* assistant—and a back up assistant for breaks. He needed constant supervision!"

"There I agree with you, Angela," Claire said, in a conciliatory tone but speaking honestly.

"What do I care about your opinion!?! Say your prayers, bitch. It is time for you to die!" She aimed her gun and Claire closed her eyes.

But just then, the door burst open. "Drop the gun, Angela!" McCoy said in his coldest, nastiest inspector voice.

But Angela didn't drop the gun. She whirled around and aimed right at him. He shot her once in the chest and she fell. Claire fell, too. She slumped to her knees and passed out on the floor from sheer adrenalin overload.

At that moment Tia, Gus and Amanda tore through the door and Gus ran to Claire screaming and sobbing. She dropped to the floor and placed Claire's head in her lap moaning and keening in a display of emotion no one had ever witnessed before from the self-centered and self-contained Gus. Meanwhile, Amanda raced over and dropped down to take Claire's pulse just as Claire's eyes fluttered open. "She's not dead!" Amanda bellowed at Gus, bellowing being necessary in order to be heard over her uproar. "Stop that racket!"

"Oh," Gus said weakly, and sat back on her heels until she realized that her right knee was giving out on her. She rose creakily to her feet and blushed, suddenly aware that she'd made a spectacle of herself.

Claire looked at her and grinned, feeling like Tom Sawyer must have felt at his *funeral*. Then she looked at McCoy. "I owe you one!" she said. "But you never would've gotten this far without me." Then Claire closed her eyes and passed out again. It had all been just too much!

Epilogue

It was two days later, Monday, the third of December, and they were all gathered for a celebratory meal at *The Three Musketeers*. When Roscoe had heard what had happened and what the profits from the restaurant's last quarter had been, he'd insisted on treating them. Lydia was also there at Claire's invitation, along with Jessie and Karen and Doreen. Everyone was happy to hear that Lydia's jaw had not been broken as badly as the doctors had first thought. The wire had been removed and she could now eat soft food as long as she was careful.

Dan began by raising his glass. "I want to make a toast to Claire, who never gives up!" Everybody raised their glasses and drank to her. Dan turned back to her then and said, "And, Claire—if you ever do anything that foolhardy again, I will divorce you and find myself a nice, docile woman who'll spend her energies looking after me and Jessie and not running around getting into trouble!"

Everyone snickered and Gus suggested that Claire tell the story from the beginning since some of those present didn't know all the details.

Claire started with the day of Pamela's murder and proceeded from there. She discussed the various leads Doreen had provided and added, "Doreen followed through on the delivery man, herself—with a little encouragement from Amanda—and then she saved me from discovery in the microwave room by pulling the fire alarm, so we decided to make her an honorary member of our team!"

Doreen looked pleased, but was then shocked when Gus described the locker caper. Lydia looked at her apologetically but Doreen just reached over and patted Lydia on the shoulder saying that she understood why it was necessary. She never would have given up the key voluntarily. Gus was uncharacteristically quiet when Claire described how she and Jessie had found her in the locker and at the end, she raised her glass and proposed a toast to Jessie. "Without her help that day, I would not *be* here," she said, her voice cracking. "Whatever else Jessie lacks, she has good hearing and good instincts." They all agreed and raised their glasses. Jessie grinned as if she understood and Claire commented, "See, Aunt Gus, Jessie likes the limelight, just like you. Everybody laughed and even Gus saw the humour in it.

After this, Amanda took over, telling a bit about her various interactions with the lunchroom students with the others chiming in to crow over what a natural she was at class control. Gus then talked about her experiences with Jessie in the drama class and how Brian had been eliminated as a suspect. There wasn't much mention of Brian's part in that whole story but Claire forgave her for that.

Tia discussed how she'd followed up on Claire's idea of a restaurant lead and found Enrico. She related how they'd connected over sharing a common Italian dialect and how he'd then given her the information about Pamela and Gustaf. "*Basta*, by the way, means *enough* in Italian, Tia explained. "It's short for *abbastanza*."

Claire interjected to say that this had been the turning point in the case. They were completely out of leads before Tia had made this discovery. She then told the end of the story and what Angela had confessed. Tia mentioned how she'd been really worried at the funeral when she saw that look in Claire's eye. McCoy had been quick to respond because he knew how Claire operated and they headed after her with Tia along to guide the way. Nobody was much interested in hearing about the tense, bloody moments that had followed and Tia saw Dan gulp.

"I had a phone call from Sergeant Crombie this morning," Tia said. Enrico is out of intensive care and it looks like he'll recover. He lost a lung though."

"But Angela is dead. She died at the scene," Claire said sadly.

"Why do you even care?" Gus asked. "Look at what she did—including planning to kill you!"

"The inspector *could* have just shot her in the arm!" Amanda interjected.

"Police are trained to shoot to kill," Dan explained. "In tight situations like that, they don't usually get a second chance."

"I just worry about Nico," Claire said. "What's going to happen to him now?"

"You said that you and Tia were going to try to visit Paolo today," Gus pointed out. "Did you do that?"

"Yes—and I got him to call Family Services. Nico's social worker is going to arrange for more support hours at home for Nico when he comes out of the hospital. And I put Paolo in touch with one of my staff members I thought would work well with Nico. She told me she'll be looking for some part-time work about that time."

"What did he say about Angela?" Lydia asked.

"It was very sad really. Paolo talked about her nightmares and how she often woke up at night crying. Despite all her denials to others, she apparently felt very guilty about drinking when she was pregnant and what it had done to Nico. She was obsessed about doing everything she could to help him, but they had a very poor relationship according to Paolo. She just did not have the right personality to deal with Nico directly and that's why she kept trying to work around him and bullying others to do the same. There was a lot of stress in the home because of Nico's behaviour and Paolo thinks that in the end, Angela just became unbalanced."

"Well, you've done what you could," Amanda said, "and more than many would have done under the circumstances. We can only hope for the best."

"Well," Jimmy interjected. "The best Dan and I are hoping for is to keep Claire and Tia out of trouble for awhile." With a flourish, he pulled four plane tickets out of his pocket and laid them on the table. "On Friday, the four of us are off to the house in Mexico for the two-week Christmas holiday."

"What?" Tia and Claire shouted in unison. "Without consulting us?"

"You don't consult us before you take some potentially life altering actions,", Dan retorted. "I guess now you can have some of your own medicine!" The others around the table snickered nervously, wondering what was coming next.

"But I have responsibilities!" Claire cried. "I can't just walk away from the group home. It's not going to run itself! And what about Jessie?"

It's all taken care of," Gus said airily. "Jessie is going to be bunking in with Mavis while you're gone so she won't be lonely. We've rented a hospital bed for her and it's actually being delivered tomorrow".

"And I'm going to take your place at the home and will be staying there while you're away," said Lydia. "My parents won't be back until after the holidays and this gives me a perfect excuse for not spending

Christmas with my sister. She's not my favourite person right now."

"What about extra staffing? You can't do it all, Lydia—and do you even feel strong enough to *do* this?"

"What I'm feeling mostly right now is bored so I'm really looking forward to this," replied Lydia. "And a couple of my friends who're very capable were looking for extra hours over Christmas, so I hired them with Jimmy's and Dan's approval. They sat in on the interviews." Jimmy and Dan grinned, both looking very pleased with themselves.

"So everything should run smoothly, and we're just across the street to help out if needed," Gus added.

"What if Bill has a melt down?" Claire asked.

"I suppose Marion could come in," Amanda suggested.

"No. She's leaving next Sunday for that long delayed trip to Scotland she's been planning," Jimmy explained. "But Bill has a really good relationship with Tom, his afternoon assistant, at this point. Tom has agreed to drop everything and come to look after Bill if there's a bad situation like that." After a pause, he added somewhat bitingly, "Don't worry. We've taken care of everything—all of it behind your back—just the way you two like to operate. We're all leaving on Friday and it's not open to debate."

"And Mario? Have you forgotten all about him, Jimmy?" Tia asked accusingly.

"No, I haven't," Jimmy replied. "Mario has been in on this since Dan and I first started discussing it a couple of weeks ago, and he fully approves of what we're doing."

Mario, himself, interjected at this point, "Yes, Mom, I think it's time you and Jim-Dad spent some quality time together alone. You never know how hectic things will be after the baby arrives."

The rest of them cracked up when they heard this and Tia just rolled her eyes. "Where are you planning to spend Christmas then?" she asked sarcastically.

"That's all been worked out with Nonno and Nonna. And I've worked out a list of activities that I think we can all enjoy doing together so the time should pass quickly."

"I wonder how thrilled they'll be after two weeks with you?" Tia muttered.

Mario just grinned. He knew his grandparents doted on him and that their general view of things was that he could do no wrong.

Claire and Tia looked at each other helplessly, and Gus raised her glass with the rest following suit. "To Claire and Tia, and a well deserved holiday!"

THE END

ABOUT THE AUTHOR

 In her private life, Emma and her husband, Joe Pivato, have raised three children—the youngest, Alexis, having multiple challenges. Their efforts to organize the best possible life for her have provided some of the background context for this book and others in the Claire Burke series. The society that the Pivatos have formed to support Alexis in her adult years is described at http://www.homewithinahome.com/Main.html.

Emma's other cozy mysteries in the Claire Burke series are entitled *Blind Sight Solution, The Crooked Knife,* and *Roscoe's Revenge.*

www.ingramcontent.com/pod-product-compliance
Lightning Source LLC
Chambersburg PA
CBHW020315260626
47156CB00004B/1240